To Kill a
PRESIDENT

MIKE SPENCE

Published by Binomial Publishers

Contact author: mikespenceauthor@gmail.com

Web: www.facebook.com/authorMikeSpence

This is a work of fiction. Names, characters, places and incidents either are the product of the author's imagination or are used fictitiously and any resemblance to actual persons, living or dead, events or locales is entirely coincidental.

A catalogue record for this book is available from the National Library of New Zealand.

ISBN 978-0-473-67424-3 (paperback)
ISBN 978-0-473-67425-0 (EPUB)

To Sue

Chapter One

The light flashed on the console of the helicopter as simultaneously a loud whoop-whoop of a warning siren could be heard through the headphones worn by all of the occupants. The white helmets of the pilot and co-pilot had the names Bob and Mary in large blue letters on the back. It was obvious that there was now some sort of emergency as Bob and Mary turned to look at each other. Joe was sure he would have felt more comfortable if the names had been more along the lines of the *Top Gun* movie. Names like 'Maverick' and 'Iceman'. Bob and Mary somehow didn't seem to fill him with confidence. The orientation flight over Vancouver had been uneventful until this point, passing over the land, sea and rafts of logs waiting to be exported from the city's vast harbour.

A cold sweat appeared on Joe's brow as the helicopter went into a steep dive. It did not seem to be a normal manoeuvre for a helicopter. A crushing grip took hold of Joe's arm. It was being exerted by the man sitting next to him. This was Inspector Brad Heke of New Zealand Police. A totally fearless bear of a man except for one thing. Flying. It was Joe who had persuaded his colleague and friend to come on the orientation flight offered by the Canadian defence force. In the event that they did not all die in a horrible ball of flames as the helicopter ploughed into the ground, he knew he was in for a hard time from his friend.

Like Joe, the emotions of the seven passengers on board surged as the helicopter dived. They represented the official government observer delegation from New Zealand to Vancouver for APEC 1997. New Zealand would host the meeting in 1999. Joe mused for half a second what the impact would be of losing the top seven officials designated to deliver the conference security in a helicopter crash at this stage. New Zealand with only a population of four and a half million did not have talent to waste.

As the helicopter dive turned into a descending corkscrew, Brad's vice-like grip on his arm strengthened. Joe thought it was entirely possible that his arm might break before they hit the ground.

The final passenger in the row of three next to Joe was Captain Clive Robertson of the New Zealand Army. He and Brad had met Clive for the first time and introduced themselves at Auckland Airport the previous day when they had boarded the direct flight to Vancouver. Clive was of average build and height, and despite a rather pronounced limp in his right leg, he would easily disappear in a crowd.

On the twelve-hour flight it soon became obvious to Clive, or any of the other passengers on the plane who cared to notice, that Brad did not enjoy flying. After Brad had pushed the attendant call button for the fourth time to get his red wine glass refilled, it was Clive who effortlessly explained to the hostess that his 'friend' did not like flying and if she would like to leave the red wine bottle they would look after him. In about two seconds she weighed up the three occupants of the seats and said, 'Well, I am not supposed to...' but, not for the last time on this flight, she placed a bottle of red wine on Brad's table and, with a hint of a smile, retreated to the back of the cabin.

The expression Joe now observed on Clive's face in the helicopter was one of interest. There was no hint of concern as he looked at the control panel and the actions of Bob and Mary. Joe's reaction was to think that this is one cool captain 'under fire' and to make two mental notes. One: do not play poker with this guy. Two: his initial description of average was not now a term he would use in the future to describe anything about Captain Clive Robertson.

Joe knew the names and designations of the other four passengers sitting in the rows behind him. But for some entirely illogical reason, it felt to Joe like it would be dangerous to turn around and look at them.

The formal introductions were to take place at a

working dinner that evening. This would be the first full meeting of the six men and one woman that made up the seven key individuals tasked with delivering the security for the APEC event in Auckland in 1999, 'APEC99'. At this point in the helicopter's spiralling descent, Joe seriously doubted that their meeting would take place.

As Bob and Mary worked the flight controls in a flurry of motion, Mary pointed to something out of the front of the helicopter. Her hand traversed across the windscreen, locked on the location as the helicopter continued to spiral down. There was the faintest of nods from Bob as the helicopter straightened out and headed for a green patch about the size of a football pitch.

As the green patch grew larger, the helicopter swooped in, more like an airplane than a helicopter. It cleared the top of a long two-storey building by a matter of metres. The nose rose to check the air speed and the machine plopped onto the grass like a duck landing on water. It was in fact a football pitch.

The voice of Bob came over the headphones to make an announcement. However, before he got to the end of his sentence to say, 'Please stay seated until the rotors have stopped turning', Brad had opened the helicopter door and was halfway out. He was now sprinting across the grass. At only a slightly slower pace, he was followed by the rest of the passengers. The last passenger out was Clive. He still had the same inquisitive expression on his face.

The passenger party moved away from the helicopter

towards the two-storey building and to where Brad was now headed, panting for breath. It was then that Joe noticed the several hundred small faces pressed against the windows looking at them. They had landed in a school playing field.

As the rotors and engine wound down and the noise subsided, Brad, still out of breath and to no one in particular, yelled, 'What the fuck was that?'

After a short silence, it was Clive who responded in a very measured tone. 'That, my friends, was an In-line Oil Debris Monitoring Alarm, more usually known as an ODM. May I also say that that was a very well executed emergency landing response to the alarm by our Canadian crew.'

Brad, after a very large breath, then levelled at Clive, and began 'What the f...' before regaining some composure to ask, 'What is an ODM?'

Clive then continued in his matter-of-fact way. 'In simple terms it is a monitor, essentially a magnet in the oil pipeline which attracts metal particles in the oil. If it attracts any particles this may be an early indication that the helicopter's gearbox is breaking up and about to fail. Hence, as our experienced pilots immediately realised, it is a very good idea to land as soon as possible.'

It was Tom Shape who asked Clive, 'Are you familiar with this type of aircraft?' Tom was the only other person on the helicopter that Joe knew well. He had worked several times with Tom on collaborative projects with the

New Zealand Security Intelligence Service – the SIS. Tom, a very high-ranking SIS officer, liked to describe his organisation as like the CIA, just a lot smaller and perfectly formed. This always amused Joe as, rather than perfectly formed, Tom himself was a little on the rotund side. However, people underestimated him at their peril. He knew Tom to have a mind like a steel trap.

Clive said, 'This helicopter is actually very new, being a variant on a family of helicopters called the Bell Iroquois, also known as a Huey. This particular one is called a Griffon CH-146 and is the Canadian-variant built in Quebec. In fact, New Zealand purchased eleven Iroquois in the late 1960s. I flew one of them last year in New Zealand; she shared the same birth year of 1967 with me.'

Joe mused that this made both the New Zealand helicopter and Clive thirty years old.

Clive went on. 'New Zealand Defence do like to get their money's worth out of defence capital spending.'

Mary had remained in the helicopter as it shut down. Clive moved to shake Bob's hand as the pilot headed towards the group. 'Thank you, Pilot.'

'You sure are welcome,' returned Bob in his Canadian drawl. 'Sorry about that lady and gentlemen. That particular alarm demands an urgent landing. This helicopter will certainly not be going anywhere until it is fully checked out. I have radioed base and they will be sending transport to take you back to your hotel.'

At that point a large woman hurried across the grass.

On seeing that everyone was alright, she smiled at the pilot and said, 'It is very nice of you to drop in but do please call ahead in future.'

Joe thought: 'I guess if you are the head teacher looking after several hundred kids, being unflappable and having a sense of humour are pretty much a job requirement.'

The trip to the Vancouver city centre hotel where the group was staying was uneventful. The Canadians had been keen to get the delegation away from the helicopter landing site as quickly as possible, and before the inevitable press arrived. The three Delta Police department-marked cars had taken the seven quiet guests back to their hotel in the CBD.

Joe was aware that there are a dozen local police departments in the greater metropolitan area of Vancouver. The Delta Police force reigned in the area where their helicopter had landed. The lead responsibility for the APEC97 event, however, would go to the national police force – the Royal Canadian Mounted Police. The world-famous RCMP has similar duties to the FBI in the USA, but also undertakes local policing duties in those provinces and areas in Canada that have no local force.

As is normal around the world with high-level overseas security observer delegations, the RCMP had appointed a senior officer to liaise, advise and generally keep members of the delegation out of trouble. Superintendent Jean-Pierre Cassel had met each member of the delegation at Vancouver Airport as they had arrived over the previous few days and escorted them, in the minivan he had been allocated for the event, to the hotel.

Because of the strain on police resources that such a major event creates, Jean-Pierre had been seconded from Montreal, some 4500 kilometres away. He was small in stature with an easy smile and the most delightful French accent to his English when he spoke. It was so charming that Joe wondered if he deliberately exaggerated it.

It was Jean-Pierre who had arranged the orientation flight with the Canadian Air Force and had driven the group to the helicopter pad located just outside of the CBD that morning. He had been waiting there for the group's return when he had been informed of the 'mishap'.

He was now waiting by the entrance to the hotel as the group disembarked from the three police cars. As he counted his seven charges, all upright with limbs attached, the easy smile returned to his face. 'Bonjour, my friends, and how were your observations?'

As he shook the hand of each member of the New Zealand delegation in turn, he explained that, as requested, a private room had been arranged in the hotel for the delegation to have their working dinner that night. After ascertaining that there were no further questions or requests for him, he announced that he would leave his charges to freshen up before dinner and would see them at nine the following morning to continue a more 'land-based' programme of meetings.

Joe headed for the hotel elevator with Brad. He pressed the button for his fourteenth-floor room and asked, 'Which floor, Brad?' Brad simply leaned across him and with a finger like a battering ram depressed the eleventh-floor button. Brad then simply glowered at him. It is difficult in a lift to try to find something to be intensely interested in order to avoid the gaze of another person, but Joe tried his best. Meanwhile Brad gave all the indications of a volcano about to explode. In a blatant attempt at deflection and self-preservation, Joe said, 'You should probably give Sharron and the girls a call.'

Brad was totally besotted with his wife and five beautiful daughters. Joe had joked with him on more than one occasion that 'Thank God the girls get their looks from their mother'. Brad was quite openly glad of this also. The deflection had some minor impact and the temperature of the volcano moved down from superhot to very hot. Joe was very relieved when Brad, without uttering a word, got off the elevator on the eleventh floor.

Joe's hotel room was one of those major chain hotel rooms that could be any chain in any major city in the world. As usual, he noted that the cleaning staff had been drilled to put every item in its allocated location within every room with an almost military precision. Any attempt to put the waste basket in a different location would, no doubt, see it return by an unseen hand within a few hours.

It was not that Joe did not like precision. His career

had revolved around it. Born and brought up in the UK, he obtained his First-Class Honours degree from Oxford University in Computer Science. He had also been able to indulge two of his other passions of playing rugby and the additional rugby social requirement of drinking beer. He had been approached while still at university by the Government Communications Headquarters. The GCHQ is a part of the alphabet soup that makes up the Five Eyes signal intelligence gathering and sharing arrangement between the USA, Canada, UK, Australia and New Zealand. The genesis of this arrangement had come about following the Second World War. The successes of the British in breaking the German codes in Europe and the Americans in breaking the Japanese codes in the Pacific had saved innumerable Allied service men and women and shortened the duration of both theatres of war considerably.

At the end of the war, this fact was not lost on the leaders of the five Allied countries and the, necessarily highly secret, signals intelligence cooperation agreement began. Despite all of the highly public disagreements that had occurred between the five countries in the intervening time, the intelligence-sharing arrangement had not missed a beat in over fifty years.

Joe had enjoyed his thirteen years with the GCHQ. After just a short period with the organisation, he had found himself managing a team of highly intelligent code breakers and technology specialists. While they had very diverse backgrounds, they had two things in common:

extremely high IQs and an almost total inability to communicate face to face with another human being. This highly challenging role set the stage for Joe's career of managing technology and the technologists.

On leaving the GCHQ, Joe had spent several years in the private sector managing large computer and telecommunications projects. Although this work had been very lucrative financially, it had not been totally fulfilling.

Now forty-one years old and following the latest in what was becoming a string of failed romantic relationships, Joe had decided a major change was in order and took the role of Director of Technology for the New Zealand Police. Joe thought it was one of the best technology roles you could have with responsibility for all telecommunications, computer systems and police radio networks in a 24/7 high-energy business covering an entire country. Joe's New Zealand citizenship had been fast-tracked with the role, not a normal occurrence, and he now carried both British and New Zealand passports.

In the job, he had also met two people who had become very good friends. Tom Shape of the SIS vetted him for the role. A top-secret security clearance was required, something Joe had held with GCHQ in the UK. In New Zealand, the SIS officer interviewing candidates is usually a crusty old former senior police officer, but for some of the more sensitive roles a more experienced SIS officer is used.

It was 4 pm when the SIS officer was shown into Joe's

office in police headquarters in Auckland to conduct the interview. Tom Shape introduced himself, and promptly announced, 'Well, it is getting late in the day, what say we conduct this interview in an establishment serving liquid refreshment?' Joe had later left the pub around 10 pm not drunk, just very, very relaxed. While never seeming to ask a direct question, Tom seemed to have elicited comments from Joe on a wide range of subjects. Often the best professionals don't even seem to be working when they are.

The first meeting with Brad had been more regular. Brad had been appointed as the police planning officer for APEC99. As a senior inspector he had the rank to make things happen. This was no easy task in the early stages of a major operation not taking place for several years. Brad knew from experience that getting senior staff to engage with the planning for a future event would be difficult. In direct contrast, as the event arrived and the political profile went through the roof, the problem would be keeping senior staff away. He knew well that if the event was a success, everyone would have been involved; and if it was a failure, it would likely have been just him, a cleaner and the tea lady from the canteen. As the saying goes, 'Success has many fathers, but failure is an orphan'.

Nine months previously Brad had come into Joe's office. Joe's first impression of the uniformed police inspector as he stood there was that there was not much light left in the doorway. As Brad had introduced himself and started to explain his planning role for APEC99, Joe, as he always did, got out his pad of paper to take notes. At this point Brad had stopped talking so suddenly that Joe had asked if anything was wrong. Brad explained that Joe was the first senior officer he had talked to who had taken notes during a conversation.

Their friendship had grown with a series of meetings and a love of rugby. Brad had introduced Joe to Sharron. She was slender with long dark hair and big brown eyes – when she turned them on her bear of a husband, he seemed to melt. His five daughters, aged from six to fifteen, were all smaller mirror images of their stunningly beautiful mother.

Brad had joined the police force at sixteen years old as a cadet police officer and had risen through the ranks to be a senior inspector. In his earlier years he had had a reputation for being a player with the ladies and a hard drinker. The former had come to a screeching halt when he met Sharron. The latter had slowed only a little.

His reputation among his colleagues was that he was fearless. He had for many years been the head of what was called 'Team Policing' in Auckland. This might more commonly be known as the riot squad. As might be expected, he led from the front when circumstances demanded.

It was later that Joe realised that very few of Brad's colleagues had been introduced to his family. The big bear was not prepared to let just anyone see how the six females in his life had him wrapped around their little fingers. Brad knew this was the case and he loved it.

Just in case anyone thought they could pigeonhole Brad, they would be surprised to find that he was also one of the longest-serving external part-time students of New Zealand's Massey University. For eight years he had been quietly completing papers towards his degree, in Botany.

Chapter Two

While the New Zealand delegation was recovering in its downtown Vancouver hotel, there were two other individuals in Vancouver that night with a keen interest in the security of the APEC meetings.

Although this woman and man had never met and they had different nationalities, they did have two things in common. They had both had a meeting with a mysterious Mr Butler in the preceding months, and they were both observing the APEC security arrangements in Vancouver for the purposes of being able to breach the security in the Malaysia APEC meeting the following year.

Laura Cosgrove, retired major of the Australian Army, was sitting on her own in the restaurant of the best five-star hotel in Vancouver's CBD. She did not mind eating alone and, in fact, preferred it. Her role as a bodyguard for the 'rich and famous' had concluded for the evening. Her current assignment was as bodyguard for a Taiwanese businessman in Vancouver to try to make money from the meetings on the fringe of the APEC conference. He was a pig of a man.

She had flown into Vancouver with him two days earlier on his private jet from Taiwan. Laura could well understand why he might need a bodyguard. Earlier that evening Laura had been standing in the corridor outside his hotel suite when a very young lady in fake fur jacket and high boots had approached. Laura had been told to expect the visitor and turned and knocked on the suite door. The businessman had opened it wearing a hotel bath robe. She tried not to think of what else he might not be wearing. He beckoned the young lady in without a word and then simply turned to Laura and said, 'That will be all until 9 am tomorrow.' He then smirked and added, 'Unless of course you would like to join us for a threesome. Or would the presence of a man cramp your style?' Laura held his gaze as she reached for the handle of the suite door and slowly closed it, leaving her charge and the young lady to conduct their business.

It was not unusual for men to think Laura was a lesbian. The short hair, athletic build and preference for wearing quite masculine clothing, even when out of uniform, had added to this misconception. It had started as a mild annoyance but then she realised that, as a junior officer in the army, it could be quite a useful defence mechanism. She could rebuff the sexual advances of men like the revolting pig she was now guarding, and the many similar ones she had met in her career. The added benefit was that these men would be prevented from any dint to their masculinity, safe in the thought that, of course, she was not interested in the great opportunity to experience the sexual ecstasy they had to offer because she was a lesbian. With the male ego left more or less intact, she could get on with her career.

It had been two years since Laura had left the army. Her last role had been as an intelligence officer attached to the Australian SAS and she had been deployed to Afghanistan. She had loved her work right up until she had been forced to resign. Her time since had been mainly undertaking bodyguard contracts. She had quickly discovered that rich people were prepared to pay large amounts to guard both their bodies and superior egos. Laura had also decided that being one of the very rich people would be far more preferable to guarding them.

Now sitting in the corner of the restaurant where she could observe all of the comings and goings, her mind turned to how she might achieve this lifestyle sooner rather than later. She was considering the events of the past few months, starting with the envelope delivered to her modest Sydney apartment by an unseen hand. It had contained 25,000 Australian dollars in cash and a simple typed note reading, '16:00hrs, 2 September 1997, swimming pool, Dubai International Hotel Terminal 3'. What was not in the note, she considered, was almost as important. There were no instructions for returning the cash if she did not want to attend. No phone numbers, return address or signature were included. The location also spelled professionalism. She had stayed at the Dubai Airport hotel in the United Arab Emirates before. As a mid to high-end hotel, it is unexceptional in almost every way except one – its location on the international side of immigration control in Dubai Airport. The hotel is designed solely for people with long connection times between flights. Passengers do not collect their luggage or pass through Customs. They simply walk through the concourse and check in to the hotel, showing their passport and onward boarding card.

It had been a simple exercise for Laura to review the Emirates airlines schedule and identify a suitable flight. The flight's final destination was unimportant. The Sydney to Oslo Emirates flight she settled on would give her an eight and a half-hour stopover in Dubai Airport, making it possible for a swim at just the right time.

The pool had been quite empty when she arrived at 3.30 pm. She commenced her lane swimming with a long easy stroke. Like so many Australians, she was a good swimmer. After thirty minutes and at exactly 4 pm, she paused at the end of her lane. To any observer she was simply someone stopping for a breather at the end of her workout. A European-looking man entered the pool and swam up to her. He had very fair skin and sensible, if rather old-fashioned, swimming shorts.

The swimmer introduced himself with very precise diction and an English accent. 'Good afternoon, Miss Cosgrove. My name is Mr Butler.' She very much doubted his name was Butler, but it was an excellent choice. It fitted the accent and suggested a position of trusted service to a higher master. However, it also represented a messenger. There would be no point taking and torturing this person for information as he was merely a servant.

'Compliments on your choice of venue,' said Laura. 'An airport is a very difficult location into which to bring a firearm, and, given our attire, there is no need for a body search to identify any hidden listening or recording devices.'

'Quite,' returned Butler, 'and may I say you have an excellent swimming style.'

'Why, thank you,' said Laura, 'but I am sure you did not invite me here to review my prowess in the swimming pool.'

Mr Butler gave a slight smile and continued: 'My employer would like to contract your services for a rather special task. While your attendance in this swimming pool suggests at least an interest on your part, I should state that if I disclose this task to you and you choose not to accept the engagement, any disclosure by you to any third party regarding the nature of the task would have rather deadly consequences for you and those around you. Having said that, I am instructed to ask you at this point if you wish to hear further details regarding the engagement.'

Laura regarded Butler carefully. The invitation, money, location of the meeting and Butler himself all suggested a high level of professionalism and commitment;

this was no amateur approach. Laura levelled her gaze at him and simply said, 'Please continue.'

Butler, without any change in tone, said matter-of-factly, 'My employer's contract is in two parts. The first part is a feasibility study into the possibility of killing the President of the United States at the APEC meeting of world leaders to be held in Kuala Lumpur, Malaysia in November next year. The feasibility study is to outline the approach, cost and your preferred method of receiving the funds. You will be paid 200,000 US dollars in cash for the completion of the feasibility study, in advance of course. If the feasibility study is accepted, then the contract will be let. You will be paid twenty percent of the fee if my employers decide to accept your proposal. The remaining eighty percent will be paid on successful completion of the contract.'

At that point the only other person in the pool completed his lane swim, performed a rather ragged tumble turn and headed back down to the other end of the pool. This gave Laura the few moments to recover from the shock of discovering that she was being asked to plan and carry out the assassination of the leader of the free world. It seemed to her that the temperature in the pool had decreased several degrees.

'Should I continue?' asked Butler.

Thinking quickly, Laura suppressed the urge to shiver and simply said, 'Please do.'

'If you wish to proceed with the feasibility study then please place a yellow flower in the lounge window of your apartment on your return to Sydney. Your *Acacia pycnantha* or golden wattle is a particular favourite of mine. If you do, then soon after you will receive an offer to provide bodyguarding services to an unimportant Taiwanese businessman who will be attending the APEC meeting in Vancouver in November. This should allow you time to undertake your research as to how the event is managed and help in formulating your methodology to complete the contract at the APEC meeting in Malaysia in the following year.

'Your feasibility study must be completed by 31 March 1998. You will be given instructions regarding its delivery. Should your proposal be accepted then you will be contacted by April 30th and you may proceed. If your proposal is not acceptable, there will be no further contact and you will, of course, retain the 200,000 dollars' initial expenses. I should also note there will be no negotiation regarding the price. The price you quote will either be acceptable or it will not.'

Butler continued: 'As I am sure you will appreciate, all communications between us will be face to face or by note. There will be no electronic or telecommunications contact in any form. I should also note that the only person you will meet with regarding this contract will be me. Should anyone else contact you and purport to be representing me... well you may wish to deal with them appropriately.'

The lane swimmer had completed his lengths and

headed for the changing room. This left Laura and Butler alone in the pool.

'If there are no questions,' he hesitated for a few seconds even though he did not expect any. 'Then I will leave you to continue your swim, and do enjoy your time in Oslo. The Viking museums in the Bygdoy area are excellent and well worth a visit. I will wish you good day.'

With that Butler walked through the pool to the nearest ladder, climbed out and headed for the changing room.

As Laura stood in the pool, it was her mind that was swimming and not her body. Not least the subtlety of the Viking museum comment. As the initial contact note had been delivered to her home in Sydney, it was a fact that these people knew where she lived. Butler had just let her know that he knew where she was going as well.

Back in the restaurant, Laura's mobile phone pinged and she snapped back to the present. It was a text message from the Pig which simply said 'URGENT'. Telling the waiter her room number and to charge the dinner, she headed to the bank of elevators at a fast walk and took the lift to the twelfth floor. On arriving at the Pig's room, the door was closed. She knocked and tensed herself for what might happen next. The door opened only slightly and the beady eyes of the Pig stared out. There was a look of absolute terror on his face. Nothing was said as he opened the door a little wider, allowing Laura to slide in to the room.

It was a large suite and she was now in the entrance

lobby. All was quiet. Having surveyed what she could see from inside the main door, she looked at the Pig. He was still wearing the bathrobe, but it was open at the front. Earlier suspicions about what he might not be wearing underneath the robe were confirmed. 'Main bedroom,' he said in a strained whisper. Laura moved to the doorway of the main bedroom.

The room was brightly lit. Her eyes moved to the large bed. Lying across it was the naked body of the young girl, the belt from his bathrobe around her neck.

The Pig, who was now standing beside her, said, 'It was an accident, an accident, you must help me, help me make this go away.'

Laura calmly said, 'First, does anyone else know?'

'No, no one. Help me. I will do anything, pay anything, but this must go away,' he pleaded.

Laura stood for a moment to collect her thoughts and consider the options. She could call this in to the Canadian police. That the Pig might spend the rest of his life in jail did not concern her in the least. The problem would be that she would be front and centre in a murder investigation during the APEC event. The chance that Mr Butler and his employers would have anything more to do with her would be zero. She did not want that to happen.

As she studied the room and with the now sweating Pig next to her, a solution to a major part of her planning for Mr Butler started to take shape.

She took the Pig into the lounge room of the suite.

'Sit!' she said, pointing to the sofa. 'I will sort this out, but I will need a big favour from you in the future.'

'Anything, anything,' he whimpered.

'Stay here, do not move from this couch. Do absolutely nothing and do not talk to anyone. Do I make myself absolutely clear?'

The terror still on his face, a nod confirmed that he did.

Laura went back into the bedroom. She took out her phone and took several pictures of the wider room and the body on the bed. It might pay to have a little insurance just in case the Pig forgot that he owed her a very big favour.

She had noticed when the large amount of luggage had been taken to the room that it included a set of golf clubs in a large, padded golf set travel bag with small wheels to allow it to be dragged. She checked the cupboard in the entrance hall, found what she was looking for and removed the golf bag and clubs from the bag.

Taking the bag to the bedroom, she laid it on the floor next to the bed. It was large enough to take the body of the young girl, who probably weighed only about forty-five kilos. Laura removed the bathrobe belt from around the girl's neck. She then dressed her in the clothes she had arrived in before rolling her body into the travel bag.

She left the bag in the bedroom and returned to the lounge. The Pig was sitting exactly where she had left him.

'I am going to dispose of the body now. I want you to

take a shower and then return to this sofa. Do not answer the phone or talk to anyone. Do I make myself clear?'

'Yes,' he replied feebly.

With that Laura returned to the bedroom and dragged the bag to the door of the suite. She opened the door and looked outside. There was no one in the corridor. She then wheeled the bag into the corridor, closed the suite door behind her and headed to the elevators.

The first elevator that arrived was empty. She pressed the button for the basement carpark. Much to her relief, the elevator did not stop at any of the intervening floors. Had other people got in she would have just smiled – only a poor lackey taking the boss's golf clubs to his car.

The lease car that came with the suite was in an oversized space by the elevator. She moved to the boot of the car; the carpark was quiet and no one was in sight. Laura opened the boot and rolled the large bag in.

She drove to the more downtrodden part of the city frequented by drug dealers and prostitutes plying their street trade. Having found a quiet alley away from the main road and with no surveillance cameras in sight, Laura dumped the body out of the bag in the alley and headed back to the hotel. The body would eventually be found by the police and would be assumed to be just another dead prostitute. Such a common occurrence in this part of town was unlikely to warrant a thorough murder investigation.

On the drive back, she decided that she would arrange for the Pig and herself to leave Vancouver on his private jet within hours. There should be nothing to connect either of them to the girl's body. The hotel did not have surveillance cameras installed so there would be no video record of the girl arriving at the hotel. While the risk of disposing of the body would not have been Laura's first choice, it had solved a key part of her plan for Mr Butler.

On getting back to the hotel carpark, Laura checked her watch. It was 2.15 am, allowing her time to sort out the Pig and make her long-planned meeting. She took the elevator back up to the twelfth floor and let herself into the Pig's suite with the card key.

When she entered the lounge the Pig was cowering on the sofa. He had followed her orders exactly.

'It is done,' she said.

'Thank you, thank you.'

'Call your pilot and tell him we will be returning to Taiwan at 9 am. I will be back in a couple of hours.'

'I will do so,' he said eagerly.

She placed the golf clubs back inside the travel bag and placed them in the cupboard. The bag would be leaving with them on the plane in a few hours. It would then be disposed of in Taiwan, just in case any forensic traces of the body remained. She knew that the hotel car and suite would be thoroughly cleaned the following morning. In a thought that sent a slight chill through Laura's body, she found herself thinking, 'Thank goodness he strangled her and did not stab her. Cleaning up blood to a forensic level would have been very laborious.'

With that Laura left the room and headed to the foyer.

The attentive bellboy asked if she wanted a cab. She nodded and in a moment was pulling away from the hotel into the cold light rain of a Vancouver November evening. She found herself looking forward to this meeting, for a number of reasons.

Chapter Three

That same evening, on the other side of downtown Vancouver from the hotel Laura was staying at, a major function was taking place in the Consulate of the Republic of Indonesia. The Indonesian Embassy was, of course, located in the Canadian capital, Ottawa. The purpose of the Vancouver Consulate and its lead diplomat, the Consulate-General, was to enhance trade between the Western Provinces of Canada and Indonesia.

It was normally a quiet and pleasant posting for a mid-level diplomat, but the Consul-General had been dreading this day for months and, despite the air conditioning in the room, he was sweating heavily. He was under no illusion that this reception party could finish his career. Many invitations to the reception had been politely declined and he had had to work very hard to try to establish an 'A'-level guest list for the evening's function. He was not sure he had succeeded. The two guests of honour had just arrived, and he was in the process of presenting the reception line of formally dressed attendees. The President of Indonesia, Suharto, and his wife were in their formal attire, and were shaking the hand of each of the guests as they were presented.

To one side of the room, and ever watchful, was the deputy head of his security team. Like many Indonesians of Javanese descent, including the President, he went by a single name. His was Rossa. All his adult life he had done the bidding of the all-powerful President Suharto. During his earlier career as a military intelligence officer, he had been based in the 'liberated' province of East Timor, dealing with the East Timorese, by whatever brutal means he liked, in order to gain information. More recently he had ascended to become a member of the President's security detail. This gave him almost unlimited power to detain and interrogate anyone on Indonesian soil if there was the faintest suspicion that they posed a threat to the President or his control on power.

As he looked closely, he reflected that the President had been in power for over thirty years now. He also knew that the power was starting to slip away. The West, led by the USA, had for years turned a blind eye to the human rights abuses in Indonesia as long as they were directed against left-leaning subjects, students or East Timorese. Provided Suharto kept Indonesia from turning communist, all was fine. That blind eye being turned was, however, predicated on the events being kept within Indonesia. The excesses of the past few years were, however, gaining more international media attention. Senior figures in the West were now having to respond to pointed questions regarding the abuses in Indonesia.

As Rossa viewed the string of second-tier dignitaries being introduced to his president, it confirmed his view that powerful people were now shunning Suharto. He thought he had been correct to meet with the intriguing Mr Butler the month before. The choice of Istanbul, Turkey had seemed particularly fitting, with Europe on one side of the city and Asia on the other, the wide Bosphorus Strait separating them.

He had stayed in a boutique hotel by Taskim Square, as directed, and, at the appointed time, had descended to the Turkish baths in the basement of the hotel. In many cities in the world a business meeting between a Christian and a Muslim in hot baths might have warranted a second look. But this was Istanbul.

The conversation was as brief and as intriguing as the note and US$20,000 he had received two weeks earlier. For him the timing was perfect. He did not intend to move into retirement on an Indonesian 'Public Service' pension. That assumed, of course, that he would survive the 'cleaning of house' that would take place when Suharto was killed, removed from power or resigned.

Rossa had accepted Mr Butler's offer. This was now his third trip to Vancouver in a matter of weeks. The first two occasions had been to liaise closely with the RCMP on all issues to do with planning for security of the Indonesian VIPs attending APEC. His questions to the

RCMP planning team regarding the security that they would supply to the President of the USA were ones the RCMP had heard from other security delegation teams also. Then, as before, they had answered as best they could, and chalked it up to one more 'country' being prissy about the possibility that someone else's president might be seen as more important than theirs.

As Rossa stood and watched another low-tier dignitary being introduced to his president, a plan was taking shape in his mind. He now knew his preferred option to include in his feasibility study for Mr Butler.

Chapter Four

That same night in Vancouver the New Zealand delegation met in the private room that the hotel had provided. The meeting would be followed by dinner. A circular table had been set for seven and, after they were all seated and in an effortless style that Joe and all of the team would come to admire, the head of New Zealand's security for APEC99, Superintendent Charles Bolt, now asked that each person formally introduce themselves. He turned to his left and looked at Brad, indicating that he should start.

'Inspector Brad Heke, Planning Officer APEC99, New Zealand Police.'

'Joe Edwards, IT Director, New Zealand Police.'

'Tom Shape, SIS, APEC99 liaison.'

'Jennifer Fletcher, SIS, here to assist Tom.'

'Captain Clive Robertson, New Zealand Army, New Zealand Defence Force liaison APEC99'.

'Sir Reginald Wright-Smith. Do call me Reggie please, Advisor to the PM APEC99.'

'Well, now we are all properly introduced, I am going to ask Reggie to give us a short explanation of what we are in for.' Superintendent Bolt turned to the man sitting to his right and with a slight smile said, 'Reggie.'

Sir Reginald Wright-Smith was the only one of the seven around the dinner table wearing a tie. As he started to speak, his tone was like pulling on a slick shirt, smooth and comfortable. This was a highly educated and confident man.

'I have been working in the Ministry of Foreign Affairs and Trade for many years and in many countries. Our esteemed Prime Minister Jim Bolger has asked me to head the government task force for the planning and delivery of the APEC99 event to be held in Auckland. I will be the liaison between yourselves, the ministry and the politicians in your task of providing security for the event. The Superintendent has asked me to give a brief overview of APEC so that we may all be on the same page, so to speak. If you let me complete a brief overview, I will then be happy to take any questions you may have.

'Asia Pacific Economic Cooperation, APEC, is an inter-governmental forum of eighteen economies. I must stress they are formally called economies and not countries because of the inclusion of Chinese-Taipei and China. As you will know, the Chinese will not sit at any table at which Taiwan is referred to as a country.

However, as I am not aware of any Chinese in our little gathering this evening, I will refer to them as countries.

'There are eighteen countries represented here in Vancouver. That means, in terms of VIPs, eighteen heads of state and their spouses, eighteen trade ministers and eighteen foreign ministers, making a grand gaggle of seventy-two internationally protected persons. With your agreement superintendent, I will let you outline the government's legal obligations regarding visitors to our country who are classified as internationally protected persons.'

The superintendent nodded and Sir Reggie continued.

'Just in case that number were not large enough for you to arrange suitable protection for, there are also three countries who are here at Vancouver as observers. They are Peru, Russia and Vietnam. If all goes to plan, they will be full members of APEC by next year, and certainly by APEC99. So the high-profile protectees will elevate from seventy-two to eighty-four VIPs.

'Unlike many international organisations, APEC has only a small, dedicated bureaucracy. This is based in Singapore. The purpose of the annual leaders meeting, as it is called, is to progress security and trade between the APEC members. Including our three soon to be added countries, this group of twenty-one countries conducts over forty-seven percent of total world trade.

'In terms of the format of the leaders meeting, this takes place over two days, usually in October or November each year. Vancouver is the fifth leaders meeting to have taken place. However, the real work is undertaken by the trade and foreign ministers during the several days before the leaders arrive in the country. Their job is to finalise the agreements between countries for the leaders to sign.

'The APEC leaders' meeting will be made up of scheduled events, such as the leaders dinner, and unscheduled events such as bilateral meetings between leaders of two countries that may be arranged at very short notice.

'I should also point out that some hosting countries' heads of states have decided that it is good politics to ask other heads of state to stay on in-country, so to speak, and enjoy a state visit following APEC. As this will put a strain on all of us following such a major event, I will be requesting the Prime Minister to issue no such invitations. I fully expect to fail in my endeavours, as the temptation for a politician to bask in the international press for just a little longer following the leaders meeting will be just too much to resist.'

At this point a series of knowing looks were exchanged around the table. Everyone knew that APEC99 would be the largest security event to have ever taken place in the southern hemisphere, let alone the largest in New Zealand history. It had just become bigger.

Sir Reggie, as Joe now liked to think of him, was a career diplomat. As such, a major distinction from a politician was that he knew when to stop talking. He recognised this was the right time and, with a tilt of his head, passed control of the meeting back to Superintendent Bolt.

Brad had known Bolt for many years and simply called him Boss. Joe thought that the Boss probably knew every one of the 9000 uniformed and 3000 civilian staff that made up the New Zealand Police. Brad had told Joe that the Boss was so well liked to the point that Brad did not know anyone who disliked him. This was unusual in the police as opinions on colleagues were usually binary in nature and freely expressed. Often a colleague was either a 'good bastard' or simply a 'bastard'. At the end of a night's drinking with Tom and Joe, Brad had explained that this universal colleague classification in the police was easily explained. A good bastard was someone who had your back. A bastard was someone who used your back to step on while elevating their own career. The three had agreed this sounded about right.

On the flight to Vancouver, Brad had also related a story to Joe from many years previously when he was a sergeant in the Communications and Control Centre, often referred to as the 111 centre, and based in a nondescript building in a suburb of Auckland. Charles Bolt was a newly minted inspector and showed up for his first night in command. Charles and his wife had recently welcomed their second child into the world. One look at his face and Brad recognised that look of near total sleep deprivation. Just what you did not need on your first night of a seven-night night shift.

Brad had shown the inspector to his office and offered

to get him a cup of coffee. On his return to the office with the cup of coffee, Brad had found the inspector in his chair with his head back, fast asleep. Brad placed the cup of coffee on the desk, went to the window that overlooked the control room and closed the blinds. He then left the office, placing a yellow Post-it on the door saying 'Do not disturb'. The inspector emerged from the office about five hours later. Charles had returned the favour a few years later when Brad was guilty of a little misdemeanour. He did not elaborate to Joe what this misdemeanour was. However, the upshot was that Brad and Charles held each other in the 'good bastard' category.

In terms of stature, Charles Bolt was, in many ways, the opposite of Brad. While Brad was big with light brown skin from his Maori heritage, Charles was of slight build with pale skin and a shock of permanently well-groomed grey hair.

Joe focused again on the meeting as Charles thanked Sir Reggie for his outline and continued: 'There are a number of small countries who are members of APEC including Brunei, Singapore, Papua New Guinea and, of course, New Zealand. New Zealand will be the first small country to host the APEC leaders' meeting. Our role will be to provide a safe and as unobtrusive as possible security environment as the circumstances and threat levels will allow. I would like to make the following brief points.

'New Zealand is under international obligations to protect the eighty-four VIPs who will attend. But beyond that, each of the twenty overseas delegations will make their own assessment of the ability of New Zealand to protect their VIPs. In many instances the lead security agency in those countries for the protection of the heads of state and senior ministers, such as the Secret Service in the USA, has a veto and is able to prevent the head of state from travelling to a country if they think it would present an unacceptable level of risk. To put it bluntly, not only do we have to provide security for APEC99 that satisfies ourselves but in the two years between now and the event occurring we have to satisfy the security delegations of the twenty countries visiting New Zealand that it will be safe for their VIPs to attend. We also need to be conscious of the fact that, while the security threat level in New Zealand is typically very low by international standards, a number of these countries attending APEC will import their own threats with them.'

The dinner was served and there was much conversation as the seven people present got to know each other better. As the dinner wound to a close, Charles Bolt and Sir Reggie announced they were going to see the Prime Minister of New Zealand, Jim Bolger. The PM had arrived that afternoon and was now at his hotel across town.

Captain Clive was due to catch up with his counterparts in the Canadian army. He had also informed the group that he would get some initial feedback on the cause of the helicopter accident. While every member of the group considered it unlikely to have been a targeted attack, this was not the sort of thing you did not investigate.

Brad announced that he and Tom had to make a quick phone call regarding one of their appointments tomorrow. 'See you two in the lobby bar in just a jiffy,' said Tom to Joe and Jennifer.

'Well, shall we?' said Joe.

'Why not?' came the response from Jennifer.

They headed out of their small dining room to a quiet corner of the hotel lobby bar. The bar was a rather dark and sterile alcove off the main lobby. They took a seat and, even though the bar was nearly empty of customers, it was a while before the waitress deigned to amble over. They looked at each other and Jennifer said to the waitress, 'Not at the moment, thanks.' The waitress turned and departed at the same glacial speed with which she had arrived. Jennifer turned to Joe and said, 'So who is Joe Edwards then?'

'You tell me. I suspect you know more about me than I do.'

'Only what is in your rather extensive file. Captain of the university rugby team, really,' Jennifer said with an impish smile.

'Then you have me at a major disadvantage because I know nothing about Jennifer Fletcher. Who is she and where is she from?'

'Did no one tell you that keeping people at a major

disadvantage is a large part of our job in the intelligence service?'

Joe looked at Jennifer and there was silence between them. But not at all an awkward one.

Tom and Brad approached the table. 'And how goes it with you two?' said Tom.

'Jennifer was just telling me her life story,' said Joe.

'Yeah, right,' said Tom. 'Well, this is a rather dismal place to have a drink. I think some serious interdepartmental liaison is called for and it should not be graced on these premises.' Joe and Brad looked at each other and said in unison, 'You can't put a price on liaison.' This was a catchphrase of Tom's they had heard many times before. It usually revolved around a few drinks at a local hostelry. After retrieving their coats to ward off the cold drizzly night, the four of them headed to a local bar, the location of which Tom had obtained from the young receptionist on the hotel desk.

Chapter Five

Breakfast the following morning had been a leisurely affair for the members of the New Zealand delegation. It gave the group a chance to talk informally and build relationships. They all knew that as the Auckland event got closer and the tensions between the political, diplomatic and security considerations moved towards boiling point, those relationships would be crucial if APEC99 was to be a success.

Joe entered the breakfast dining room and spotted Sir Reggie, Tom and Clive sitting at a table. As he walked over, he cast his eyes around the room to see if another member of the delegation was there. She was nowhere in sight.

As he joined his three colleagues, Tom said, 'Oh, Jennifer had an early meeting with our cousins in the US Secret Service.'

Joe said nothing but wondered if Tom ever missed anything at all that happened in a room.

Clive announced to the table: 'Our Canadian defence force friends tell me that their preliminary findings are that the emergency in the helicopter yesterday was a faulty sensor. They are continuing to investigate but it looks like we were not the target of a sinister international plot.'

Tom chimed in: 'So this coffee is supposed to taste like this and not the result of poison?'

Clive smiled at him. 'No, you should be safe with your morning caffeine fix.'

The conversation turned to the latest tensions in the Middle East. Tom asked Sir Reggie what his take was on the end game with Iran. Sir Reggie thought for a moment. A lifetime of working in diplomatic circles had taught him that you never hurry an answer to any question, even in the most informal of settings.

'My view is that it is likely to be a matter of containment rather than solution. Despite the best efforts of Western governments and heavy sanctions, the religious fervour of the revolution remains high. It is always possible to make political arguments regarding the direction of a country, but these will simply not fly in the face of a leadership dominated by religion. It is very difficult to argue economics against religion in such an environment.'

While Joe and Tom contemplated this, Clive raised his eyes from his bacon and eggs and simply said, 'Well, I think we should just nuke them till their eyes glow.'

In the closest that they would ever hear from Sir Reggie that might be classed as a spontaneous utterance, he simply said, 'Oh my gosh.'

Tom remarked, 'And there, my friends, we have the diplomatic and military positions.'

The waitress approached and topped up the four coffees on the table. Joe said to Sir Reggie, 'On a point a little closer to our joint task, we all understand the threat to VIPs, but the APEC meetings also attract considerable demonstrations. In simple terms what are they demonstrating about?'

Sir Reggie responded in his even tone. 'Well, APEC is essentially about free trade; globalisation if you will. There are those who think that global free trade is not a good idea and that it puts too much power in the hands of large corporates, the anti-globalists. Then there are those who see it as an opportunity to protest against authoritarian leaders that may not often travel outside the safety of their own country, such as Suharto of Indonesia or Jiang Zemin of China. Of course, there are also those who simply want to protest about something. We usually group them under the heading of anarchists.'

'So,' said Tom, 'do you think there will be trouble during the meeting at the University of British Columbia this afternoon?'

Sir Reggie thought for a moment. 'Given the violence meted out by the Suharto government to the student population in his own country, I would think a demonstration is very much on the cards.'

Clive chipped in again. 'I wonder which genius thought it would be a good idea to hold a leader's lunch on a student campus with only a few roads in and out?'

The table fell silent. It was now 9 am and Sir Reggie excused himself. He was meeting with the New Zealand prime minister again to try to arrange a bilateral meeting with the USA. With Jennifer already ensconced with the US Secret Service for the day, the other five members of the group were being escorted by Superintendent Cassel. They were to inspect the arrangements put in place for the 3000 members of the world press who were covering the event in Vancouver. Later in the day they would observe the lunch meeting for the country leaders at the University of British Columbia on the outskirts of Vancouver.

The first stop for the group was at the press centre. The APEC leaders' meeting attracted press from around the world. All had to be accredited and had to wear their passes at all times. The 'media centre', as it was known, was in a large downtown conference hall kitted out to cater for the needs of an increasingly digital world press. As Brad and Joe walked around the outside of the building, they came across a Royal Canadian Mounted Police officer patrolling with his Labrador dog. At this point Superintendent Cassel joined them, showed his identification to the officer and introduced Brad and Joe.

'Not that I think it would be a high-priority target, but have you completed your bomb sweep of the media centre?' asked Cassel. The officer weighed up his three fellow police officers and said, 'No, sir, I am not allowed in the media centre.' He let that sink in and just before any of the three of them had the courage to ask the obvious question, he stated, as the smile grew larger on his face, 'You see, we don't have enough bomb detector dogs in the whole of Canada to cover all of the venues and hotels. Prince here is actually a drug detector dog.' By now all four of them were smiling.

'So your role is to give comfort to the journos that they are getting protection as befits their profession as purveyors of truth and wisdom?' said Brad.

'Yes, sir,' said the Mountie, 'but I am under strict instructions not to enter the centre. If the world journalists here are anything like the Canadian journalists for smoking weed, then Prince here is likely to front one of them and start barking like mad.'

'So,' chipped in Superintendent Cassel, 'rather than risk an international incident by arresting one of the world's press, you are out here putting on a show.'

'You got it, sir.' After handshakes all round, the three of them left Prince and the Mountie to continue their show.

Much later, at the end of a long day, Joe, Brad and Tom settled in again to the bar they had been at the night before.

'What a shambles,' said Brad, not for the first time that day.

Joe and Tom nodded in agreement. The main leaders meeting, the formal meeting of the heads of government attending, had taken place in the Great Hall of the Museum of Anthropology in the heart of the University of British Columbia. The meeting and the lunch that followed had been a success. The problem had started as the eighteen motorcades had been about to return their VIPs to the hotels. Student protestors had blocked all of the roads out of the university. Their main demand appeared to be that Suharto should be held by the Canadian authorities for crimes against humanity. As an internationally protected person visiting Canada, that was not going to happen.

The embarrassment factor of having the motorcades delayed had led 'someone' to instruct an RCMP sergeant to clear one of the roads by any means. Backed by a large contingent of police and a can of pepper spray about the size of a fire extinguisher, he had sprayed the sitting students blocking the road. The police contingent had then moved through and pushed the several hundred protestors off the side of the road. All of this was, of course, under the gaze of the world's press and would lead the news in many countries around the world.

After another drink of his beer, Brad broke the silence that had descended on the table. 'I will tell you what will happen now. A notable member of the Canadian public service, probably a retired judge, will be tasked by the Canadian government to head a commission of enquiry. That enquiry will cost tens of millions of dollars and will come out and say "Poor choice of venue and the cops overreacted". What it will not disclose is who from the government pressured the poor old Mountie sergeant to clear the road.' Silence once more descended on the table.

Tom announced to neither of them in particular, 'Of course, the beautiful Jennifer has spent the day with the American Secret Service. I would think it would have been most informative to observe their reaction when they realised that Bill was effectively trapped and the motorcade could not move. All thirty-six vehicles in his motorcade.' Tom knew that Brad and Joe would also have counted the vehicles in the motorcade as it went past them at the university.

Brad said, 'When the event takes place in Auckland, the US motorcade will be the longest and most difficult to cater for. Given the small size of the Auckland CBD, if the President's hotel and a venue he is to visit are too close to each other, the first car in the motorcade could arrive at the venue before the last car has left his hotel!'

As they all knew, there are two basic types of movement of a high threat level VIP. The unannounced, whereby if the movement is unpublicised then long-term planning by a 'bad actor' is not going to have occurred. If, however, the movement, location, arrival date and time of the VIP is known well in advance, the risk of a highly planned attack is much higher. Just ask Margaret Thatcher. She was very nearly killed by a bomb in her hotel as she attended the Conservative Party conference in Brighton, England in 1984. A long-delay time bomb, having been planted in the hotel weeks before the event, killed five people and only just missed her and her entire cabinet.

Tom spoke again. 'Subject to there being no more distractions like today, Jennifer has arranged for us to meet with the APEC99 point team from the Secret Service tomorrow. These will be the boys and girls who will undertake the planning for the Auckland jamboree in two years' time.'

'Speak of the devil,' said Tom, and they all turned to find Jennifer crossing the bar towards them.

'Good evening, gentlemen,' said Jennifer. 'And how go the interagency deliberations?'

Joe could be deluding himself, but he felt a warmth in Jennifer's smile when she looked at him.

Chapter Six

Another keen observer of the events on the University of British Columbia campus that day had been a casually dressed Indonesian man carrying a large camera. In his role with the Indonesian presidential security detail, Rossa had cleverly arranged to be detailed to monitor any student protests. Officially he was there to try to identify any students protesting against President Suharto who might be Indonesian. He would take photographs of any likely candidates and then check them against the details of all Indonesian students attending the university that were held at the consulate. 'Follow-up action' could then be taken when the students next returned to Indonesian soil.

However, he had his own variation on his official orders that would take precedence. He had focused on a group of three young students who sat together on the road faced by the police. From their looks the three could well be Indonesian. They obviously knew each other from the way they conversed. He was too far away to hear the language they were speaking or any accents. He would take his photographs and look for an opportunity to find out.

As the old police sergeant approached the sitting students carrying his tank of pepper spray, Rossa saw that an opportunity might be about to unfold and he positioned himself to the side of the road.

The sergeant let fly with the pepper spray into the sitting students and, as they choked on the acrid substance, they were forcefully moved to the side of the road by the line of approaching police. Rossa saw his opportunity and moved to 'help' the three young students with their eyes streaming as they gasped for breath.

'Can I help?' he said to the group in English. Indonesian might have put the group on their guard. He handed them the bottle of water he was carrying. 'Splash this on your face,' he said to the young girl he had given the water to. She did this and then handed the bottle to one of her friends.

'Where are you guys from?' Rossa asked.

'I am from Indonesia,' the girl spluttered, 'as is my, my friend'. She pointed to the young man next to her. She then pointed to the third member of the group. 'Ahmed is from Malaysia.' Rossa looked at Ahmed, a very slight young boy. The bottle of water had reached him and he was pouring what was left on his face. Rossa turned his attention back to the two Indonesians. Ahmed, as a foreign national, would be no good for his plans. However, the two Indonesians could be just who he was looking for.

Their photographs would not appear in the set of images he would supply to the consulate for review. He would quietly conduct his own review on these two and find their names and all personal details held by the consulate. There was no need for further dialogue at this stage. No need to alarm them or wait for the inevitable questions they would ask him when they had composed themselves. He wished them luck and walked away. A significant piece of the feasibility study he would produce for the mysterious Mr Butler had just fallen into place.

As he moved away the first of the motorcades carrying its VIPs came slowly down the now cleared road leaving the university campus. With the smell of pepper spray still in the air, the media turned their cameras from the students to the approaching limousines.

At the same time far away in Malaysia, two anxious parents were watching CNN, in particular 'Live news from Vancouver'. It was the early hours of the morning for them as they scanned the images on the television for any sight of their son Ahmed. When the TV picture of the three students suffering from the effects of pepper spray appeared on the television, the mother gasped. The father leant forward in his chair. He was relieved to see his son safe but curious as he thought he recognised the man in the picture giving the students a bottle of water.

Chapter Seven

The day following the debacle at the university, the seven members of the New Zealand security delegation met with the US Secret Service agents who would be in charge of planning for the US President's visit to Auckland in 1999. While they had also been introduced to the security planning officers for some other countries, including China and Russia, as representatives of the only remaining superpower, the US President and his massive entourage would eclipse all others. The whole New Zealand security delegation team knew that if they could satisfy the Secret Service as to the security arrangements for APEC99, they could likely satisfy all countries.

The meeting was to be quite short and informal. It was really just a chance for them to put names to faces. They had booked a small conference room in the hotel where the delegation was staying. Jennifer, as the only person who knew everyone in the room, started the introductions. 'Gentlemen,' she said, 'may I introduce Peter Timmons and Beauford Clark, both Special Agents of the United States Secret Service. Beauford here will be in charge of the US Secret Service planning for the APEC99 event in Auckland, aided by the more than capable Mr Timmons.'

There was a round of handshakes and introductions.

When Beauford shook hands with Brad, the whole room noticed they were of a similar big and powerful build. Beauford commented with a smile to Brad, 'You must be one of those New Zealand rugby players I hear about. I played American Football in college myself. Similar, I think.'

Brad smiled back as he said, 'Yes, but we just don't need all the baby padding and helmets.'

As the meeting progressed with small talk, the only slightly smaller Special Agent Timmons slipped into the conversation: 'I hear you New Zealand cops do not carry guns. Don't mind if we bring ours, do you?' He was correct, of course. New Zealand Police was very proud of the fact that it had never been a requirement to carry firearms as a matter of routine policing. Superintendent Bolt had been waiting for this to be raised. He knew that this would be a potential 'show stopper' for the US Secret Service. There was no way they were going to allow a US President on foreign soil if the Secret Service security detail around him were not armed.

Charles took the early-warning comment from Peter in the spirit that it was made and responded, 'Yes, access to firearms for visiting delegation security teams will certainly be something we will need to address.' The point had been made and registered by all.

After some further small talk Charles Bolt closed the meeting by inviting the two Secret Service agents to visit New Zealand at any time and that he would provide them with the contact details of all members of the New Zealand security team to get the communications under way.

While it was still two years until APEC99 would commence, the scale of the operation left no one in doubt regarding the work that had to be completed.

In the following four days the delegation attended a number of 'after action' briefings involving RCMP, Vancouver City Police, Canadian Defence department and others. The main talking point had of course been the student action at the University of British Columbia.

In an attempt to make light of the incident and in response to an off-camera question from a UBC radio reporter, an unapologetic Canadian Prime Minister Chrétien brushed off the pepper-spray incident by saying, 'For me, pepper, I put it on my plate.' This had not gone down well and the public pressure for a RCMP complaints' commission to investigate the incident was mounting.

The New Zealand prime minister had asked Sir

Reggie to return to New Zealand with him and they had left a few days earlier. Joe had found himself wondering about Jennifer and, as casually as he could in the car on the way to the airport, he had asked Tom where she was. Tom, who had not been fooled for a moment by the casualness of the question, had said, 'She is off to play with the cousins for a few months.' The 'cousins' was a term used regularly in the UK and some British Commonwealth countries to describe the Americans. It, of course, implied a sort of distant family member.

Chapter Eight

Rossa had returned to Jakarta with all of the information to progress his proposal for Mr Butler. He had covertly matched the photographs of the two Indonesian students to those held in the Vancouver Consulate office. He was now in possession of their names and home addresses. It had been straightforward for him to then investigate further and get detailed information on both of their families and background. There had been no need to bring anyone into his confidence. At this stage he would not. When the task was completed, he would need to disappear with no loose ends.

With the two Indonesian students he needed to make a decision. Would his primary asset be the girl or the boy? After reviewing all of the information, he decided on the girl. Easier to control, he thought. As for the boy, well, he had a very special role for him to play also.

He had obtained a new typewriter and typed the five

pages of his proposal. There would be no digital footprint of this document on a computer for anyone to track down. When he had finished the proposal, he took a hammer to the typewriter in his garage and placed the many pieces with his household garbage. There would be no matching the keys of a typewriter either. The proposal would be the first and only document typed on this typewriter.

At the end of March an envelope had arrived for him at his home. It simply contained a ticket for a performance of the Jakarta Wayang, better known in the West as shadow puppets, on the night of 31 March.

The shadow puppets show was not something that interested him, but it seemed a very good venue for the purpose this evening. A few minutes before the end, with house lights dimmed and the show on the stage having reach a particularly high crescendo of noise, he took the small envelope from his pocket. Keeping his hand low by his thigh, he handed it to the pale-skinned gentleman in the evening jacket who sat next to him. The Englishman, who he had met for the first time in Istanbul, slid the envelope into the event programme he held in his other hand. This was all completed without either of them moving their heads.

Rossa had thought long and hard about the amount he would propose to complete the task. The statement that there would be no negotiation on price placed the onus on him to make his requirement 'reasonable'. He had settled on ten million US dollars and included that with the numbers for a Swiss bank account. This seemed like a nice round number to him.

The Asian financial crisis was savaging Indonesia. President Suharto's position was becoming more tenuous as each day passed and, with it, Rossa's own position in the personal protection detail. His movement into retirement might come sooner than he had thought. All he had to do now was wait and see if his offer was accepted.

Chapter Nine

Laura Cosgrove had also been busy. It had been easy for her to turn down the few bodyguarding jobs she had been offered. The research she had needed to complete had been accomplished through the use of Sydney's many public libraries. She had only ever visited one library per day, and she had never needed to visit the same library twice. She had made use of the public computer terminals connected to the internet available at the libraries. If the nature of her internet searches had tripped interest from any of those signals intelligence agencies that monitor such things, there would be no real pattern to follow. There would also not be a recurring internet address to lead them to the person conducting the searches.

Her research had focused on aircraft types and munitions. Also, the history of the war in Afghanistan and the eventual defeat of the Russian forces, primarily due to them losing their dominant control of the skies.

The other part of her work had involved meeting up with her former colleagues. A reunion dinner with her old friends from the SAS had provided the perfect opportunity to sound out a particular friend. He had recently returned from a deployment to Afghanistan. This was very hush-hush. As far as the Australian public knew, there were no Australian soldiers serving in Afghanistan at this time. Their official deployment there would follow a lengthy and well-coordinated campaign to convince the Australian public of the merits of the endeavour. The conversation with the returned detachment members had turned to the mess left when the Russians had withdrawn from the country and the even bigger mess left by the Americans. They had flooded the area with weapons and ammunition, including some very sophisticated anti-aircraft weaponry. The aim had been to help the local population deal with the armoured Russian helicopters that, for years, had owned the skies and rained death and destruction on the Afghanis below.

After a few drinks the opportunity presented itself to talk one on one with her friend. Captain Alexander Conrad was the senior pilot attached to the SAS. It was his role to fly detachments of SAS in and out of some of the most dangerous places in the world. As might be expected of arguably Australia's best pilot, either helicopter or transport plane, he was very good at his job.

Laura had done most of the talking, projecting onto

him how unhappy she was working as a bodyguard for rich pricks. How badly treated she had been by the Australian defence force and that there were opportunities in the private sector that could pay a lot of money. Nothing explicit was said, but Alex knew exactly where she was heading. She was positioning him for an offer further down the road. His level of agreement to her statements confirmed he would be interested in such an offer.

Following the evening with her former colleagues, Laura had written her proposal for Mr Butler. She had purchased a second-hand personal computer and printer for the purpose from a local market. She knew from her military intelligence training with the special forces that, in order to delete all electronic traces of her document from the computer, she would need to extract the computer hard drive and destroy it.

Just after completing the proposal, a ticket arrived in the post for a performance of Puccini's *Turandot* at the Sydney Opera House.

Dressed in her best evening dress and clutching a purse – in fact her only evening dress and purse – she had attended the performance, taking her seat about five minutes before the opera was due to commence. As was usual, the Sydney Opera House was packed.

To her right sat two elderly Australian ladies. The seat to her left by the aisle was empty. As she pretended to study the performance programme, a man came and sat in the seat next to her. She turned to look at him, and he gave her a polite nod. It was not Mr Butler. Her mind started to race, and she recalled clearly Butler's instruction that only he would contact her. Should she leave now? Should she engage the unknown man in conversation? It was unlikely that any harm could befall her in a packed opera house with the lights full. However, when the house lights were dimmed, her risk would increase considerably. It was now about three minutes until the performance started. She decided the best course of action would be to leave before the lights dimmed.

At that moment she heard someone with a perfect English accent say to the man seated next to her, 'Excuse me, sir, but I believe that you may be in my seat.'

She glanced casually to her left to see Mr Butler in a perfectly fitting tuxedo showing his seat ticket to the man next to her. The man took his ticket from his pocket and, after checking the seat number, apologised to Butler, and he stood and headed towards the back of the theatre.

Butler took his seat and, turning to Laura, said, 'That is an easy mistake for someone to make.' They exchanged that slight smile that strangers sitting next to each other do. At that point the house lights dimmed, the curtain rose and the performance commenced.

Sometime later, with the audience enthralled and the Italian tenor arriving at the climax of the signature aria 'Nessun Dorma', she had gently slipped the envelope from her purse to the hand of the very well-dressed gentleman sitting next to her. As the audience rose to their feet to applaud the Italian tenor's very loud efforts, Laura thought how apt. *Nessun dorma* translates to 'Let no one sleep'.

Chapter Ten

When Joe and the group had returned to New Zealand, Superintendent Bolt, with Brad's encouragement, had decided that they should move out of their separate offices in various police stations around Auckland and move to a suite of offices exclusively for the growing planning team. Suitable offices had been found above the Post Office in central Auckland and the team members had started to move in. Tom, Jennifer and Sir Reggie would attend the monthly meetings but, as they were seconded to New Zealand Police from other agencies, they would remain based at their own offices. Captain Clive had arranged to be deployed full time as defence liaison to the planning team for the two years until the event occurred. He had moved into the office next to Brad.

The political scene had been equally busy in New Zealand since their return. Prime Minister Jim Bolger had spent a lot of time out of the country, at the Commonwealth Heads of Government Meeting in Scotland in October and then at the APEC Meeting in Vancouver in November. During these absences, his transport minister had been particularly busy. Not on matters to do with her official portfolio but on widening the divisions in her own party. She had obtained the support of enough colleagues in the caucus to replace Bolger as prime minister. On 8 December 1997, barely two weeks after having returned from the APEC leaders' meeting in Vancouver, Jim Bolger decided to resign rather than face a vote of no confidence that he knew he would lose. He was replaced by Jennifer Shipley, who would become New Zealand's first woman prime minister.

Prime Minister Shipley had wasted no time in summoning Sir Reggie and Superintendent Bolt to a meeting in her Wellington office before Christmas had even arrived. She was well aware of the unique opportunity for her to shine on the world stage that the APEC meeting in Auckland would offer. Sir Reggie and the Superintendent left the meeting under no illusions about the effect a failure would have on their careers.

Joe enjoyed the new offices and working each day with his friend Brad. Support staff had been added, but the plan was to keep the overall planning team small and manageable.

By April Joe had detailed plans on the thirteen technology projects that he wished to put in place for the event. The projects ranged from radio communications to computer systems. There were two key factors that made the planning for these systems different from any other systems development work that Joe had ever undertaken. First, the lifetime of the systems was only about ten days, from the minor dignitaries arriving to the heads of state departing. Second, the projects had to not only work but, in the year and a half that now existed before the event started, he would need to convince visiting security delegations from around the world that, like the other components of the security plan, the technology that would be in place to protect their respective heads of state was international best practice or above. No small feat for a small country off the end of the world with a population of 4.5 million, plus, of course, 45 million or so sheep.

His task today was 'simple'. He had to convince the three senior officials from the New Zealand Treasury that they should give him the budget of NZ$35,100,000 that he wanted for the projects. Police had for a number of years been soaking money out of Treasury for a massive pet computer project of the Police Commissioner. Joe had told the Commissioner that the project in its current form and design would fail. In simple terms there are two ways to develop a major corporate infrastructure IT system. Evolutionary, where you implement a function one at a time and allow the business and the computer system to grow together. Or revolutionary, where you ask the organisation to stop growing or changing while you install your IT system. The Commissioner had chosen the revolutionary approach. He was having about as much success at stopping his organisation from growing and changing as King Knut had had in stopping the tide from coming in. The net result was that the project's costs were completely blowing out and Treasury was, quite rightly, very sceptical that good money should not be thrown after bad.

Given this climate, Joe was now asking Treasury for $35 million for IT projects in Police for a ten-day event. It was not going to be easy.

The three senior Treasury officials that now sat opposite Joe looked more like a firing squad. Treasury officials have a reputation, even among other civil servants, for being dour and emotionless, a view not dispelled by speeches from the Governor of the Reserve Bank.

Joe opened up with the signature IT project among the thirteen he was asking funding for. This was a major enhancement on the rudimentary computerised Command and Control system that Joe had seen in operation in Vancouver.

'You have got to be joking,' was the opening line of the red-faced Treasury official at the centre of the firing squad. Any illusion Joe had that he would sell the projects on their merits evaporated. He would need a new strategy.

The Boss had been relating a story to him from the previous week's monthly update meeting with the prime minister that he and Sir Reggie attended. As one of the civil servants was explaining a minor matter, Prime Minister Shipley had seemed uninterested and was browsing some unrelated papers. The official noted that the minor issue had not yet been resolved and that a committee would be looking into it. At this point Shipley's head snapped up and she fixed the official with a stare. She stated very categorically: 'By the end of the day I want a name. I want the name of the person who will resolve this issue. There will be no responsibilities left with committees regarding the APEC meeting. If any matter should be unresolved regarding APEC, I will personally speak with the individual responsible.'

The message was very clear. If you wished to progress your career in government then do not mess up on this, and no typical civil service ploy of handing off a problem issue to a faceless 'committee' was going to be allowed.

Back in Joe's meeting, the three Treasury officials had 'taken aim and fired' as Joe explained each of the major projects and its place in the overall plan. Joe had taken each volley of shots and simply moved on to the next project. After they had finished discussing the last of the projects and, by way of closing the meeting, the Treasury official at the centre of the three announced, 'We will consider your funding request and will respond in due course with our decision.' With that the three then started to rise from their seats.

Joe, in the most even, unassuming and non-threatening manner he could muster, asked, 'Just before you go, gentlemen, can I make sure that I have the spelling of your names correct?'

The three hovered for a moment and then returned to their seats. Joe continued: 'In the event that, for example a head of state does not attend the APEC meeting because they consider the technology component of the security arrangements are not up to scratch, I will of course need to supply a report to the Prime Minister's Office.'

Joe tried not to smile as each of the officials spelt out their name and Joe noted it on his pad.

Two days later a letter from the Treasury arrived confirming that all the projects would be funded in full, as requested.

Chapter Eleven

Laura had spent April in Sydney waiting to hear from Mr Butler. It is one of the most pleasant months in Sydney as the excessive heat of the summer dies away. She had not really noticed the weather as she waited for the response to her proposal. She had turned down a couple of lucrative bodyguarding jobs since her trip to the opera and filled her days running in the park and going to the gym. She had stayed away from any meetings of substance.

There had been one diversion with a short trip to Auckland to meet up with her friend. They had decided that their relationship should remain a secret. She had considered telling him about Butler and her plans but dismissed the idea. Too risky for both of them and not appropriate yet. She resolved to tell him if she got the contract. She owed him that.

Waiting was not one of her strong points. During

extended periods of inaction her mind would start replaying the events in Afghanistan that had led to her parting company with the Australian defence force.

It had started simply enough. The officer in charge of the Australian SAS detachment, a lieutenant colonel, tended to stand a little too close to her. Or, if viewing something over her shoulder on her computer screen, he would place a casual hand on her back. This was something she had dealt with several times in her career. Right or wrong, she now saw it simply as an occupational hazard.

Following the loss of a helicopter with its three crew and four members of his SAS unit to Taliban ground fire, the detachment commander had become more withdrawn. With the cumulative stress of the deployment, he had become what was termed in defence force circles as a 'hollowed-out' man. In the following days she could smell whisky on his breath as he stood even closer to her in the operations room.

She had woken that night in her bedroom on the airbase to find him on top of her. His face was just centimetres from hers and, terrifyingly, showed no expression at all. He was nearly twice her weight and, with one hand over her mouth and the other tearing at her clothes, she seemed powerless to move him, even with all of her training. As the huge hand over her mouth moved and stopped her breathing through her nose, she feared she was going to die.

She kept her service pistol in its holster between the

bed and the bedroom wall. Even though they were on a secure base, a Taliban attack could happen at any time. The thought of being captured by the Taliban was a frightening thought for a man, but for a woman! It had never occurred to her that she would need the pistol to defend herself from one of her own. As she could feel herself losing consciousness, she slid her hand between the bed and the wall, frantically searching for the pistol. Just as she was despairing, she managed to grip the pistol and snap it up. Placing it to the side of his head, she pulled the trigger. His body was now a dead weight slumped on her. To this day she is still not sure if she caught him by surprise or if he saw the pistol being put to his head and did not care.

The response of her senior officers to the incident had been swift and efficient. That a troop commander they had appointed to a key command position could have acted in such a manner would be a black mark on all of their records. This had been a highly decorated officer in a hugely sensitive and politically explosive role.

Laura was given a choice. She could face a very messy court martial for the murder of an 'unarmed' senior officer. She was aware that there was no guarantee that she would be acquitted, but it would be certain to end her career. The second choice was to sign a statement that she had responded to the sound of a gunshot and found her commanding officer had committed suicide. She would then be permitted to resign 'honourably' with all benefits and pension intact.

Laura reasoned that either way her career was over so why risk a prolonged and stressful court martial? The army had no doubt that Laura would keep the matter secret as she would have provided a false sworn statement regarding the incident.

As she had always done to deal with an extended time of waiting, she threw herself into physical exercise. It was late April when she was running her favourite route around the Sydney Royal Botanic Garden, Government House and the Domain, a route with spectacular views of the Sydney harbour. These were views that she never noticed with the speed and effort of her run. She was on her second circuit when she saw him. Mr Butler was sitting on a bench close to the famous viewpoint called Mrs Macquaric's Chair.

She ran past for about 200 metres to see if anyone else of interest was nearby. Satisfied that there was no one out of the ordinary, she slowed and headed back to the bench. When she arrived, she placed her foot on it and started to unnecessarily adjust her shoelace.

'Your running style is as effortless as your swimming style, Laura,' said Butter.

'Why, thank you once again, Mr Butler.'

'I regret to inform you that your proposal has not been accepted by my employers.' Butler paused but Laura made no comment. 'It would seem very unlikely that we will meet again. However, may I wish you a long, happy and safe life.'

With that Butler smiled at her, the way a grandfather

might smile at his grandchild, rose and ambled slowly down the path.

As she changed legs resting on the bench and, again, unnecessarily retied her other shoelace, she had two immediate emotions: deep disappointment that she would not be joining the ranks of the very rich anytime soon, and a chilling feeling. The intent of the final sentence had been unmistakable.

Still, she had spent her life keeping secrets and, while this was a big one, it was just one more to keep. She would follow the news from the APEC leaders' meeting later in the year in Kuala Lumpur with added interest. But, for now, she would need to make some phone calls and see if any of those bodyguarding contracts she had turned down were still available.

Chapter Twelve

Rossa had spent his time since delivering his proposal to Mr Butler in Jakarta on ever more frantic efforts to protect President Suharto. The mood around the Indonesian leader could best be described as 'dead man walking'. There was rioting in the streets and several students had been killed in the protests.

The handwritten message delivered to Rossa at his home arrived at the end of April. It was short and simple: 'Tomorrow, National Museum, 11.30 am, Chinese Ceramics'.

As Rossa entered the museum, he thought it was another good choice of venue for a meeting. With all of the foreign tourists around, a pale-skinned gentleman would not attract as much attention as he might in a café or restaurant. It was 11.25 am as he made his way to the ceramics collection.

He walked over to a large glass case containing some

exquisite painted vases and stood next to the European gentleman in the suit who appeared to be studying the contents of the exhibit intently.

'Do you know that your National Museum contains one of the finest collections of early Chinese ceramics outside of China?' said Mr Butler.

'No, I did not know that,' Rossa casually responded, as if making conversation with a complete stranger.

Butler turned his gaze from the colourful vases, looked at Rossa and smiled. 'I can confirm that your proposal has been accepted. Please proceed and ... execute.'

It was Rossa's turn to smile as he asked, 'And the funds?'

'If you confirm you are able to proceed, the two million dollars initial payment will be deposited into your Swiss bank this afternoon.'

'I will proceed,' said Rossa. With that the well-dressed European gentleman smiled once more, gave a slight nod of the head and casually walked away.

That evening Rossa called his Swiss bank and, after relaying the account number and his security information, they confirmed that the balance in the account was US\$2 million. Twenty percent of his contract fee had been paid.

The following day he resigned from his role with the presidential security team. He would need more time to conduct his business, and it would be better to get out now and not wait for the inevitable turmoil when Suharto departed. There was no need to work any notice period as he had months of long service leave to take. His resignation did not sound any alarm bells as he was one of many Suharto 'loyalists' jumping ship at this point.

On 21 May 1998, three weeks after Rossa resigned, Suharto succumbed to the pressure placed on him from all sides. After thirty-one years as president of the fourth most populated country in the world and having wielded absolute power for most of that reign, he resigned. He was quickly replaced by his vice-president Doctor B.J. Habibie.

The civil and political turmoil in Jakarta only served to assist Rossa in the work he now had to do. Old political scores were being settled and new political and power alliances created.

Chapter Thirteen

As 1998 progressed, the pressure on all the New Zealand planning team increased. Overlaid on this was the constant requirement to brief the security staff of major countries as to the arrangements being put in place. The allocation of the hotels for the leaders to stay at was also a major issue. Not only were the security arrangements critical but there were other 'political sensitivities' to cater for. The hotel for the Chinese had to be bigger and better than that for Taiwan. The Korean delegation would not share a hotel with the Japanese.

Peter Timmons and Beauford Clark of the US Secret Service made three visits to New Zealand. They had listened to the presentations regarding security for the US and asked appropriate questions. Joe and Brad had taken them on site visits to four potential CBD hotels for the president to stay at. Ideally, they wanted an entire hotel for themselves. The favourite had been the Stamford

Plaza at the lower end of Albert Street in the city. It ticked most of the boxes for New Zealand Police and the Secret Service. One lighter moment during the inspection of the hotel occurred as they were entering the hotel. Joe and Brad both spotted a problem immediately and, as a smile broke out on both their faces, they stopped walking and Brad said in his best theatrical manner, 'Oh, no.'

Peter and Beauford both stopped in their tracks and let their gaze roam around to identify the problem. Their professional pride would not allow members of a foreign police force, no matter how professional and easy to work with, to identify a security risk before they did.

The Secret Service not only has the role to protect the physical security of the president but they are also required to protect him from embarrassment. With Bill Clinton being the current occupant of the Oval Office, and the details of his affair with Monica Lewinsky being daily fodder for the world press, this was no easy task. As the four of them stood in front of the large glass walls and doors that form the entrance to the hotel, Brad announced: 'For the President's arrival we will close the street, erect barricades on the far side of the street and create an area behind the barricades for the press.'

Brad went on to an attentive audience. 'So as Bill gets out of the car, about where we are standing now, he will turn to wave at the press.' Brad theatrically performed a presidential wave towards the other side of the street. He then changed his wave to a pointing finger and slowly turned 180 degrees and pointed at the glass façade. 'They all take their photograph of the arriving President Clinton, and the backdrop is...?' he teasingly asked.

The two Secret Service agents looked through the glass façade. Beauford said quietly, 'Oh, no.' Clearly visible at the back of the foyer was a small shop beneath a large sign that said 'Cigar Shop'. They could all clearly see the headline that would appear in newspapers around the world. 'US President arrives in New Zealand and heads straight into a cigar shop.'

A brief moment elapsed until Brad said, 'No problem; we will take care of that.'

An issue of less brevity and the only really major sticking point with the Secret Service at this point was the carrying of firearms. One of the problems with the discussions on this topic was that, as North Americans, Beauford and Peter could not understand how this could be an issue. However, in New Zealand, police officers do not routinely carry firearms on patrol. Also, although shotguns and hunting rifles might be commonplace in the rural communities, handguns are virtually non-existent. The New Zealand public would not take kindly to seeing armed foreigners on their streets. Brad had been given the task of solving this problem. If it could not be fixed, it was in the potential 'show-stopper' category.

Events such as APEC meetings base their security on the threat level in the location at that particular point in time. The threat level is based on all intelligence available. VIPs naturally have different threat levels at various times. A meeting of twenty-one heads of state had the added threat of being a significant potential terrorist target. Peter and Beauford had been surprised, and rather delighted, to find that New Zealand had only suffered one terrorist attack in its history. They were even more surprised to find out it was undertaken by the French government, at the height of French nuclear weapons testing in the South Pacific in 1985.

Like a lot of people in the region, New Zealanders were outraged at the French actions. Greenpeace had based one of its ships, the *Rainbow Warrior*, in Auckland. This ship had had some success in sailing into the proposed test explosion areas and causing delays and, more importantly, helping to focus international attention. The response of the French government was to despatch agents of its intelligence service to Auckland to sink it. An explosive device was attached to the ship and it was sunk in Auckland harbour on 10 July 1985. One member of the Greenpeace crew was killed. Two of the perpetrators were caught by the New Zealand Police and, after a trial, imprisoned for the attack. The French government then blackmailed New Zealand using international trade threats. After the intervention of the UN Secretary General, agreement was reached to allow the man and woman to complete their sentences on a French island in the Pacific. The French, in flagrant disregard for the agreement, quickly repatriated the man back to Paris on the pretext of a health problem. He was followed shortly afterwards by the woman when she became pregnant. As Brad pointed out, 'They were obviously not holding her in solitary confinement.' Just in case there was any doubt left at the total arrogance of the French in the criminal actions they committed on New Zealand soil, they subsequently awarded both individuals medals.

While the action had taken place thirteen years earlier, there was some relief in New Zealand that, as France was not a member of APEC, they would not be attending the meeting in Auckland.

Joe and Brad had surprised their American guests in another discussion. Peter had been explaining the American preference, when meetings such as this took place on islands, to station a number of navy ships off the coast to provide helicopter support and fighter air cover, if necessary. Joe had explained that the transit times for the aircraft would be rather long as the ships would have to stay outside the 200-mile territorial limit. As Peter and Beauford shared a perplexed look, Brad had explained that in 1984 New Zealand had declared itself to be nuclear free. As it was US Navy policy to neither confirm nor deny if any of its vessels were carrying nuclear weapons, all US navy vessels had been banned from New Zealand waters.

When Peter asked playfully how Joe and Brad thought New Zealand would fare if the most powerful navy the world had ever known decided to steam into a New Zealand harbour, Brad had warned him that we had several waka, Maori war canoes. In the event of a conflict, they would fiercely paddle out to meet them. All in the room agreed that in light of this likely 'stalemate of forces', an alternative would need to be found.

As the APEC leaders' meeting in Kuala Lumpur came closer, Joe continued to manage into place the thirteen major projects for the event. Circumstances demanded that each of the projects was leading-edge. The problem with leading-edge IT projects is that the sharp edge is very dangerous and can cause major damage to one's career prospects. The major project was the creation of a Command and Control centre with suitable physical and technical resilience to house the three-shift control room staff that would man the location 24/7 during the event. Other projects were high-definition television with a microwave downlink fitted to the police helicopters and GPS locators fitted to all police vehicles to be used in the motorcades. The latter had never been done before but would greatly assist in the 'choreography' that would be required to move twenty-one simultaneous motorcades around Auckland. The APEC event would also require a dedicated computer system for the collection and dissemination of all information. Joe was quite exhilarated at being involved in these projects. However, he also recognised what the cost of failure would be.

Between the long hours of work, Joe had managed to meet up with Jennifer a few times. He liked her. She was very smart and had an impish sense of humour. But with the long hours he worked, and the strange hours she worked, catching up on a regular basis had not been easy. She had no mobile phone, and all Joe could do was leave a message on her 'company' voicemail and ask her to call back.

It often took a week before she called back. When, at one of their dinners, he had casually asked why it took her so long to return his calls, she said straight away, 'Well, I get so many offers to go out to dinner, I was just waiting to see if I got a better one.'

'Serves me right for asking.'

For Joe, it just added to the mystery of the woman he found very alluring.

As befitted her profession, she was an expert at deflecting questions. One of the few facts that Joe had ascertained was at the end of one of their dinners. When it came time to pay, a very light-hearted discussion had ensued with Jennifer saying she did not feel it necessary to pay half of the bill as Joe had eaten twice as much as her.

She then proceeded to allocate weights and costs to the entire content of the three-course meal they had consumed and, in her head, calculate the appropriate percentage cost for each of them for the dinner.

When she had finished, Joe had simply given a round of applause and asked, 'How did you do that?'

'The benefit of having a first-class honours degree in Applied Statistics.'

They had smiled at each other as they both knew that Jennifer had shared something personal with him.

Chapter Fourteen

It was now the beginning of November 1998 and only two weeks until the leaders' meeting in Kuala Lumpur. Rossa had finished all his preparation work and now was the time for the action to begin.

The detailed research on the two Indonesian students from Vancouver had confirmed what he had hoped for. They were both from comfortable middle-class homes in Jakarta. They had no significant political connections. It would not do for him to be successful in his task only to find out that powerful forces in Jakarta would take an undue interest in his actions. The girl had two younger brothers who lived with their parents in a small house on the outskirts of the city.

Rossa had taken a one-year lease on a secure upper-price-bracket apartment in Kuala Lumpur and had come and gone without incident over the last six months. The

Malaysians and the Indonesians often refer to each other as brothers. They share a lengthy land border on the island of Borneo and both are Muslim-majority countries. For all appearances, Rossa had been just one more Indonesian businessman working in Malaysia.

The significant item he needed had been created for him by an old army colleague in Jakarta. His now ex-colleague, an armaments specialist, had lost a hand in East Timor while removing a mine. The irony of the situation was that the mine had been placed by the Indonesian army to try to eliminate East Timorese freedom fighters who patrolled in that area. The accident had left the man not only with the loss of his hand but also his job in the army.

The man had always seemed a little too bold in his work. Rossa had recalled a comment made to him many years before. 'There are old bomb disposal experts and there are bold bomb disposal experts, but there are no old bold bomb disposal experts.'

He was now trying to scratch a living on a very meagre pension. The offer of a significant sum of money for the creation of the unusual device had been readily accepted.

On completion of the device, it had taken Rossa two days to move it from Jakarta to his apartment in KL. While the many daily flights between the cities only take two hours, he had not risked even the lax security screening at Jakarta Airport. Instead he had chosen to take one of the ferries that connect the two countries, not exactly a first-class experience but no one asks any questions and baggage is never searched.

Rossa then had the luxury of taking a short flight back to Jakarta. He had one more item to attend to before he headed off to Vancouver.

For years under Suharto the Indonesian army had been using gangs of thugs to break up student protests or union meetings. One such gang organiser was now sitting opposite Rossa at a quiet coffee house in one of the more well-to-do suburbs of the city. No introductions were necessary as the two men had conducted 'business' in the past. Rossa handed an envelope over the table.

'As usual, half now and half on completion of the exercise,' said Rossa.

The 'as usual' comment by Rossa was quite deliberate, so that the man might think this was 'government' business as in the past and that could only be helpful.

The man picked up the envelope and flicked through the large wad of Indonesian rupiah that it contained. He extracted a small piece of paper from the envelope. It contained an address and four names, under the heading husband, wife and two sons.

He raised his eyes from the list and said, 'This address befits their place in our society. No additional complications?'

The gang lord recognised the address as a lower middle-class suburb of the sprawling city of Jakarta, unlikely to house people of great wealth, power or political connections.

'It does and no additional complications,' Rossa replied.

'Hold, scare or worse?' was the next enquiry from the man.

'Hold for ransom and supply me with a telephone number that I can use to talk with them at any time.'

'And when would you like this to happen?'

'Next Wednesday evening.'

No more words were spoken as Rossa got up and left.

Rossa arrived in Vancouver on a tourist visa the following day. There was no diplomatic passport any more as had been the case when he was part of Suharto's security team. There would be no contact with the Indonesian consulate either. He hired a car from the airport and spent three days observing the two young Indonesian students he'd selected at the university campus riot. They were still friends with the Malaysian boy and the three of them dined together each evening. Having decided on his course of action, he went into a local hardware store and purchased a spade, paying cash and placing it in the boot of his car.

It was simple enough to approach the Indonesian boy when he was alone on campus. The boy had not recognised him at first as the man who had helped him and his friends during the student protest the previous November. A reminder and a smile from Rossa and trust was built between them. The offer of a lift in his car across campus was gratefully accepted.

He left it three days before approaching the girl. By then she had reported to the campus police that her friend was missing. They had taken the details but shown little concern. Students went missing all the time. Her concern, however, was rising with each passing hour.

Rossa decided to approach her in the university library where she had chosen a quiet corner. He could see that she was not concentrating on the books in front of her. She recognised him as he approached but there was no smile from either of them. She could feel the menace in his stare.

'Say nothing and just listen to me. Your family is in extreme danger. I have some photographs to show you,' he said in the Javanese dialect that he knew they both spoke. He placed a photograph of her missing friend in front of her. Her eyes widened but she said nothing.

He then said, 'Your friend's family were kidnapped and he did not do as he was told. This was the result. He handed her a second photograph. It showed her friend lying in a shallow grave, his face bloodied and broken. She gasped and looked from the photograph to the man sitting opposite her. Her emotions were taking over and then through the fog in her mind she heard the quiet voice of Rossa.

'I need you to remain calm. There is someone I need you to listen to. If you make a scene they will be hurt.'

He placed his phone in her hand and, on the table in front of her, he put another photograph. As she looked at the image in the photograph a voice filled her head. She recognised the voice, but it seemed to make no sense. As the horror in her rose, she gasped loudly. Her arm was resting on the table and the man sitting opposite placed his hand on it, appearing to anyone watching as gentle and caring. He said in a hushed tone, 'Quietly.' She looked at him and then back at the photo in front of her.

Her father, mother and two brothers were sitting upright on four chairs in a room she did not recognise. The chairs had been put together in a line. She could see the ropes binding them to the chairs and the gags around the mouths of her mother and brothers.

Over the phone the man had given her, the girl could hear her father calling out to her, pleading with her repeatedly, 'Just do what they say, please just do what they say.'

Rossa gently took the phone from her hand.

'I need you to come with me now and ensure that your family is returned safe to your home.'

The girl looked at Rossa but made no move. Rossa picked up her backpack and slowly placed her belongings spread around the desk in it. Collecting the photographs on the table and putting the girl's rucksack over his shoulder, he gently placed his hand on her arm and said, 'We must go now and save your family.' With that the girl rose and they left the library.

As Rossa pulled the car away from the parking spot outside the hall of residence and headed towards Vancouver Airport, he was pleased with his work so far that day. As he had calculated, he had applied just enough terror to make the girl compliant without putting her over the edge. His tone had been calm as he had explained to her that they would be flying back to Jakarta to save her family. She did not yet know that they would have a stopover in Kuala Lumpur on the way through. He would constantly reinforce that the safety of her family depended solely on her.

They had returned to her room in the hall of residence to collect her passport and a few clothes. He had made her take a sleeping tablet. This should take full effect during the flight. If it kicked in a little early, well, she was just one more drowsy passenger getting on a flight. He had booked two business class seats. She would be by the window with him next to her in the aisle.

He drove into the rental car return space in Vancouver Airport terminal and dropped his car keys in the return box. He left the slightly muddy once-used spade in the boot of the car.

As the car had pulled away from the hall of residence, neither of the occupants had noticed the Malaysian boy coming down the footpath. He had been coming to visit his friend. They had become even closer over the last few days as their concern had risen for the missing third member of their group. He saw her strained face in the front seat of the car first and started to raise his hand to wave. Then he recognised the driver of the car and froze. Why would she be driving off with this man? The reason he remembered the man so well after a year was that his father had asked about him after the trouble at the university during the APEC meeting the previous November. He froze for a moment as the car headed down the road. Then he knew what he had to do and took his phone from his pocket.

Chapter Fifteen

The same seven members of the New Zealand security observer delegation that had first met as a group in Vancouver almost exactly a year ago had now all arrived at their hotel in Kuala Lumpur. The hotel was called somewhat underwhelmingly The Mines. It was two days until the leaders meeting. Most of the official activity was centred around a rather more opulently named five-star hotel, the Palace of the Golden Horses. The Palace together with The Mines and some other hotels, shopping centres and amusement parks had been built around what was once the world's largest open-cast tin mine. The enormous pit was now a beautiful lake and its location some thirty-five kilometres south of KL's CBD was a showcase for Malaysian development. The Prime Minister of Malaysia, Dr Mahathir bin Mohamad, host of this APEC meeting, intended to show it off.

Dr Mahathir had been prime minister for seven years

and had steered Malaysia through considerable economic growth and around the rocks of the Asian financial crisis on which his fellow head of state to the south, Suharto, had foundered.

Many, including inside Malaysia, viewed him as a strong leader driving his country forward. To the West he was an authoritarian tyrant constraining democracy and the rule of law. His relationship with the old colonial masters, the UK, and the new economic colonial masters, the USA, were openly hostile. APEC presented him with a 'once in a generation' opportunity to place himself, and of course Malaysia, at the centre of the world stage.

The New Zealand team had again been provided with a minibus and a dedicated guide. If one could imagine the opposite of the knowledgeable, professional and affable RCMP Superintendent Cassel from the Vancouver trip, this would have been the incongruously named Dominic, corporal of the Royal Malaysian Police Force.

The portent of things to come had been set when Dominic had collected Brad, Clive and Joe from KL Airport. As the three had exited Customs, they identified the uniformed corporal holding a sign bearing their names. Unfortunately, the sign was upside down. Brad sat in the front of the minibus and attempted to engage Dominic in conversation. Through Dominic's limited English, it became apparent that Dominic was not from Kuala Lumpur but from 'somewhere else' in Malaysia. This was further confirmed when, part way into the journey, Dominic's swivelling head movements indicated that he had no idea where he was. Nothing was said between the three of them as Brad extracted a KL street map from the side pocket of the van and took up the navigation duties; it was a role he was to play for the rest of the visit.

The first official visit of the group had been to the Command and Control headquarters of the Malaysian Police. It became apparent during the visit that when they said Command and Control they meant it literally. Most police forces in the world devolve responsibility to area commanders who utilise a local radio network to deal with police matters in their region. These range from the mundane to the serious.

In Malaysia, police command and control is highly centralised in the KL headquarters. Here there was a dedicated radio operator for each and every police radio network across the whole of Malaysia, the shift commander proudly informed the group. In the event that a civil disturbance is identified in any of Malaysia's thirteen states, then the shift commander in KL can respond. This can include, if necessary, deploying police parachutists to assist local officers.

The Mines hotel was a decent four-star hotel on the edge of the lake. It had a large swimming pool and an artificial beach covered in rough coral sand that had been placed between the swimming pool and the lake. Although it looked very inviting, swimming in the lake was not recommended as tin deposits and other toxic chemicals continued to leach into the water from the decades of mining.

The pace of their visits was a lot slower on this trip than Vancouver. The senior Malaysian police officers were very focused on the event management. A mistake under the command of any officer would likely result in immediate dismissal. On the other hand, nursemaiding an observation team from a small country at the bottom of the Pacific was unlikely to enhance one's career. Also, the model used by the Canadians was closer to that which would be adopted by New Zealand. It was intelligence-based and policed with the help of the local community. The Malaysian approach was to flood the area with thousands of members of the police and army. There would be no demonstrations by any groups as it was known that this would not be tolerated. At the first sign of any sort of gathering, it would be broken up and ringleaders hauled off to prison. If they were lucky, they would be released when the event was well and truly over.

It was 3 pm and a few of their group were away on meetings related to their specialities. The next major item on their joint agenda would be the arrival of the US President on Air Force One later that evening. Joe, Jennifer, Brad and Tom had decided to have an afternoon by the hotel 'beach'. The boys had been in the pool when Jennifer arrived. Joe found himself watching as she slipped off the colourful sarong she had purchased in a local market and laid it on one of the loungers by the pool. She was wearing a light blue swimsuit that perfectly hugged her trim figure. Joe's eyes had not left her as she turned to come down the steps into the pool. As she swam towards them, Joe turned back to his two friends. They were both staring right at him with smiles on their faces.

'What?' said Joe. They continued to smile and said nothing as Jennifer swam up to the group.

After a little while Joe and Jennifer decided to join an impromptu game of beach volleyball that had started up next to the pool. Brad and Tom thought this a bit too much effort in the heat of a KL afternoon and retreated to two loungers in the shade.

The players on the volleyball court were a mixed bunch of nationalities, shapes and sizes. A member of the resort staff in a bright yellow T-shirt was acting as referee and trying, but not too hard, to bring some semblance of order to the game. Joe and Jennifer's deep-seated competitive spirits were to the fore as they threw themselves around the sand court. As Joe dived down on the rough coral sand to try to save a well-spiked ball from the opposition, he felt his knee cap scrape the surface. The ball found the in-court area and the opposition all cheered and high-fived. As Joe got to his feet, Jennifer noticed the red knee with a hint of blood starting to flow.

'Deary me,' she said in a mocking tone to Joe, 'have we scraped our kneeses?'

Joe responded in kind. 'Nothing we rough, tough rugby players can't handle.'

Jennifer, with a change in tone, said, 'You know coral sand cuts can be quite infectious.'

Joe said nothing and just looked at her.

'I have some antiseptic cream in my room. Come on.'

'Sounds very sensible to me,' said Joe. They headed off to the loungers by the pool where they had left their clothes and towels, scooped them up and headed to the hotel block containing Jennifer's room. During the short walk, Joe studiously did not look in the direction of Brad and Tom, who, he knew, would not have missed a thing.

They entered Jennifer's room and, as she closed the door behind them, she put a finger to her lips and pointed around the room. Joe nodded. This was a reminder that the room was highly likely to be bugged. Jennifer had not bothered to check for the bugs. It was standard protocol when a member of the intelligence services visited a foreign country, 'in the open' rather than under a false identity, to assume that their hotel room would be bugged by the local intelligence services.

'Sit down and I'll get the ointment,' said Jennifer.

She returned from the bathroom, knelt down on the floor by Joe's feet and, after dabbing the knee with a wet cloth, applied the ointment. Joe winced slightly with the sting from the antiseptic cream. Looking up at him, Jennifer mockingly said, 'Roughy-toughy rugby player, there, there, all done.'

With their eyes locked on each other, Joe matter-of-factly said in a rather staged voice, 'Well, I think I should be going now.'

He rose and went to the door. He turned and, staring again at Jennifer, he opened the door. Without taking his eyes off Jennifer, he then closed it with a loud thud while he remained inside the room. He then walked quietly into the bathroom, slid off his shirt and, still wearing his swimming shorts, opened the large glass door and stepped into the shower cubicle. Leaving the door open, he turned on the shower. He turned to see Jennifer enter the bathroom while simultaneously undoing her sarong, which fell to the floor. Still wearing the tight-fitting blue swimsuit, she entered the shower. Joe placed his hands gently on her shoulders as his hands moved to slide the thin straps of the swimsuit over her shoulders. Joe leaned in and whispered in her ear, 'Now, exactly what secrets do you think we can reveal?'

Chapter Sixteen

In his apartment across town from The Mines hotel, Rossa was preparing for the coming evening. Many times he had pushed a detained suspect up to and, on occasions, over the edge. He had done what was necessary to extract information that may be of interest. Occasionally, he had just needed to confirm that the subject did not know anything of interest. His work with the girl had been a variation on this past practice. He needed her to be functioning and compliant, so applied just the right amount of terror. Although she was shocked to be stopping over in KL, Rossa was glad to discover that she was smart enough to understand the gravity of both her and her family's situation.

They had not left the apartment since arriving the previous day from the airport. He had stocked up with everything they would need for their short stay. He would let the girl talk again with her father before they left.

The phone call with her father had the right effect on the girl. The fact that she was now closer to them, KL being so much closer to Jakarta than Vancouver, gave her some hope. She was getting closer to home, closer to saving her family.

Rossa had explained to her that her parents had been taken for a ransom. That when they returned to Jakarta she would be expected to collect the ransom from her father's bank. When the money was paid to the kidnappers, they would all be freed. It was a lie, of course, but in her state of fear it was something to grab hold of – like a drowning person grabbing a life ring. Rossa knew that he had to keep just the right mixture of fear and hope in the girl.

While she was still reeling from talking with her father, Rossa had announced that they were going to KL Airport for the flight to Jakarta.

They would have to do one small job at the airport before they got on the plane. He was to photograph an important person. She would need to appear as his assistant and so would need to wear a media photographer's jacket. Her mind was still reeling, but the important thing was that they were on their way to the airport, and her home and family in Jakarta.

Rossa produced a brown sleeveless jacket covered in pockets and told the girl to put it on. There was a small badge on the front that said 'PRESS'. The six large pockets on the front of the vest each bulged. As she undid the Velcro strip to look in a pocket, it revealed a large camera lens. She assumed the other pockets must also contain lenses.

'Just leave the pockets alone,' said Rossa quickly. 'They are there to make to you look like a press photographer's assistant.'

The girl looked at Rossa, but his eyes did not invite questions. Rossa moved towards the door. The two small suitcases that they had brought with them from Canada were there. They each picked up a suitcase, left the apartment and headed towards the elevator and carpark in the basement. They were on their way home to save her family. Nothing else really mattered to the girl.

They drove in silence to the airport and Rossa parked the car in the space for the rental returns. He extracted the two suitcases from the boot along with a large SLR camera. After dropping the car keys in the fast return box by the parking bay, they headed for the departure lounge.

The airport was busier than the girl had ever seen at any airport. Police officers and army soldiers seemed to be everywhere. They looked up at the departure board and she saw that a Garuda airlines flight for Jakarta was leaving in just over three hours. The check-in desk was number 43.

Her heart raced with this confirmation that they were headed for the flight home. As they arrived at check-in, Rossa said, 'Wait here, I will check us in,' and, taking her small suitcase and passport, he strode down the first-class check-in lane. The lady at the counter was just opening up. However, as Rossa arrived she turned on the welcoming smile. Rossa's back was to the girl as he handed over the documents. The girl heard the attendant say, 'Two items to check in, sir?' To which she saw Rossa nod. After a moment, the two cases trundled up the conveyor belt and the attendant returned the documents to Rossa with 'Enjoy your flight, sir.'

Rossa turned to the girl and placed the documents in his pocket. The only item he was now carrying was the camera. For the first time in three days the girl felt a flash of optimism. She was indeed on her way home.

Rossa's emotion at that time was one of satisfaction. The last small subterfuge had been played out. The girl would not be travelling with him on this flight or on any flight in the future. He had in fact just checked in himself and both suitcases under his name. There was no record of any booking for the girl as there never had been one. Any security video of the check-in process would also show that he checked in alone. This was the last 'ray of hope' he would need to shine on the girl to get her to do his bidding.

Rossa, with the slightest nod of his head, indicated to the girl that he wanted her to follow him. He walked from the departure area to the arrivals and then to an area under a large flight of stairs. He knew from his previous reconnoitring of the airport that this location was not covered by the security cameras. The girl followed him.

'Wear this,' he said, pulling from his pocket two plastic wallets on lanyards. He placed one over the girl's head and the other around his own neck. The girl looked at it, noticing that it was an 'APEC Press' pass complete with her photograph on it.

'This will get us to where we can get a good picture,' he said.

It had been a simple exercise to get the press passes a few weeks earlier, A few forged documents, a photograph of each of them and the five US$100 bills pinned between the first and second pages of the APEC press application form he had handed over to the Malaysian accreditation official. It was not the first 'gratuity' that the official had taken to expedite a press pass. He slid the $500 into his pocket and gave the documents the most cursory of looks before stamping and signing them. He had then printed out the two small plastic passes and handed them over to Rossa.

Rossa now hung the camera he had been carrying around the girl's neck. She looked at the camera and back at Rossa. He gave her back her passport in case she needed it for the security check and then looked her over. He was pleased with what he saw. She now looked as she should, a young keen press photographer here to cover the arrival of the President of the United States into Malaysia.

Her head was spinning but she consoled herself with the thought that she would soon be on the flight home to Jakarta. She would do anything this man asked to ensure that her family would be released and they could all be together again.

At the same time that Rossa was placing the camera around the girl's neck, a group of seven observers and a local police corporal passed by the staircase. The passes worn by the seven New Zealand officials said 'APEC observer' and had been acquired through more official channels.

Brad had had to provide minimum navigation for Dominic to get them to the airport. Even Dominic could not miss all of the new road signs pointing the way to the airport. Joe and Jennifer were keeping their actions in the group very professional. Not too close to each other and not too far apart. Brad and Tom had not asked any difficult questions and, if they did, Joe would not say. The group headed across the arrivals hall to a gate marked VIP Arrivals. Everything about it looked new, including the X-ray scanning machine and metal detector gate.

Two smartly dressed police officers were the first to halt the progress of the group. They closely reviewed the accreditation pass hung around the neck of each member of the group and politely pointed them to the conveyor belt at the start of the X-ray machine. Dominic had peeled off the back of the group and was no longer with them.

On noticing he had gone, Brad said to Tom, 'We will probably see him back at the van, if he can find it.'

Although the group would not be getting on a flight today, the security process to get to the secure VIP greeting area was the same that air travellers around the world were used to. The group moved through the check swiftly and headed for the door that led outside to the tarmac.

Following a few metres behind them was Rossa and

the girl. Rossa gestured for the girl to go first before waiting for a few people to pass him while he pretended to take a telephone call. He then joined the queue for the initial check of their credentials.

He watched as one of the two police staff at the gate checked the girl's pass. He was quickly satisfied that it was genuine, which of course it was, and waved her to the X-ray machine. The female member of staff approached her and requested that she put her camera and jacket in the plastic tray to be scanned. Rossa watched as it headed off on the conveyor belt to be consumed by the X-ray machine. The helpful officer asked if she had any other metal objects in her pockets. The girl did not initially respond, and the officer asked a second time. After what seemed like an age to Rossa, the girl said no, and the officer invited her to go through the metal detector.

Rossa was placing his mobile phone and loose change in the tray for scanning when he saw the operator on the other side of the machine extract the now scanned jacket with the bulging pockets from the tray. This was what he was expecting. The operator of the scanner, if they had been paying attention, would have identified six metal cylinders of various sizes that the X-ray had not penetrated. A nod to her colleague would have indicated to him that a physical search of the jacket, and the contents of the pockets, was required.

As Rossa progressed past the metal detector, he could see the airport security official open one of the Velcro-secured pockets and extract the camera lens from within.

He turned it to look at it and then, satisfied it was a lens, returned it to the pocket. He undid each of the other five pockets in turn to discover that each contained another lens of a different size. Satisfied, he placed the jacket back in the tray and, with the camera, pushed it along the metal runners at the end of the conveyor belt before inviting the girl to collect her belongings.

Neither the girl nor Rossa noticed the slightly built, well-dressed man standing quietly by the wall of the security checkpoint area. He was studying the two photographs in his hand. Years of experience allowed him to weigh up the situation instantly. He spoke his orders quietly into the lapel microphone of his expensive suit.

With an almost imperceptible sigh of relief, Rossa moved towards the output end of the X-ray machine to collect his own few belongings. If the X-ray operator had taken all six lenses out of the girl's jacket at the same time, he might have noticed that the jacket itself was still quite heavy. The plastic explosive had been rolled into two thin sheets and expertly crafted into the front lining of the jacket. At four kilos, anyone picking up the jacket on its own might be suspicious of the weight. However, with six bulging pockets containing large camera lenses, the weight would give no cause for concern.

Each of the fake camera lenses contained hundreds of small steel ball bearings. The largest of them also contained a detonator, a small amount of plastic explosive and a radio-controlled device linked to Rossa's phone.

When Rossa sent the signal from his phone the

detonator would trigger the main charge within the vest. The resulting explosion would send thousands of metal projectiles at supersonic speed in the direction that the wearer of the vest was facing.

He and his one-handed ex-army colleague had spent two days experimenting in an out of the way place far from Jakarta. They had placed life-sized plywood body shapes at varying distances around the blast. The device would always be a compromise between weight and effectiveness. It was, after all, going to be a fairly small girl wearing it.

Settling on a configuration containing four kilograms of plastic explosive and the six tubes packed with ball bearings, they had conducted their final test. The holes ripped through the plywood body shapes had indicated that anyone within sixty metres of the blast would very likely die. The kill zone. Out to 100 metres would cause serious injury, if you were lucky.

Rossa regretted that he had to shoot his ex-army colleague in the head when he had completed his task and delivered the final version of the device, but this was no time for loose ends.

The device represented a rather more sophisticated version of the Claymore mine. This type of mine was used extensively by American forces in Vietnam and is what is known as a 'directional mine'. Forged into the front of the mines are the words 'Front Towards Enemy'.

The girl exited the security check and headed onto the tarmac through a door marked 'VIP Viewing Area'. Rossa followed and, quickening his pace very slightly, he caught up with the girl. He ushered her gently to the area cordoned off for the press and then moved to the front of the area. Just a thin rope separated them from the red carpet twenty metres away. He gently told the girl to stay there and take a photograph of every person who came down the red carpet. He told her that as soon as they had finished, they would both be on the plane to Jakarta and reunited with her parents.

The reception dignitaries were arriving at the end of the red carpet, waiting for the arrival of the President of the USA. A large roar at the end of the runway announced the arrival of Air Force One, a large Boeing 747 aircraft extensively modified and one of a number of identical planes. A common misconception is that the plane is called Air Force One. This is actually the radio call sign used by whichever plane is carrying the President.

As the plane touched down and started to taxi to the precise location to allow the President to exit onto the red carpet and the waiting dignitaries, Rossa looked around for his safe location. He would need to be about 150 metres behind the girl. This would be well within the range of his mobile phone detonating trigger but far enough away to prevent him from being injured in the blast. He would also need line of sight so he could detonate at the precise moment that the President passed close to the girl.

Rossa moved slowly and steadily to the back of the crowd and found a concrete staircase. He climbed five steps and turned to see the aircraft come to a stop and the aircraft stairs being wheeled into position by the plane. There were about six people on the concrete staircase with Rossa, all trying to get a better look at the arrival of the President of the USA.

As a figure arrived in the open doorway of the plane, he waved to the assembled dignitaries and members of the world media. A murmur went up around the crowd. Standing in the doorway was not the President of the USA but the unmistakable figure of Vice-President Al Gore.

Rossa's mind raced. There was no time to call for instructions on how to proceed, even if he had a contact number, which he did not. The contract was for the president not for the vice-president. As Al Gore started to descend the steps to the waiting dignitaries, Rossa came to a decision. The girl knew too much, and he would not be able to extract her from the airport without considerable risk. Also, he may be paid some money for killing the vice-president. So he would proceed. At about the same time that he arrived at the decision, a slender man ascended the steps and stood in front of him. Some part of his mind suggested that he knew this man and he looked more closely at him.

The man caught his gaze and returned it with a gentle smile. Rossa knew he needed to concentrate on the progress of the vice-president who was now at the foot of the airplane stairs. Then he realised why the face looked familiar. He did not know this man but someone who looked very much like him, the Malaysian boy from Vancouver. At that exact moment two large men appeared on each side of him. They put a strong arm under each shoulder and, with their other arm, took hold of each wrist. At the same time Rossa felt a prick in his neck, as though he had been stung by a bee. It was not a bee, but another man standing directly behind Rossa had expertly stuck a hypodermic needle in his neck and emptied the content of the syringe into his bloodstream.

Rossa felt himself go very warm. He looked in turn at the man on each side of him who were both supporting him and restraining him at the same time. He turned his gaze back to the man in front who resembled the Malaysian boy from Vancouver. The gentle smile remained on this man's face as Rossa's eyes closed and his heart stopped.

The gentle smile on Colonel Musa's face melted away, replaced by no expression at all, as befitted the head of the Royal Malaysian Police anti-terrorism unit, known as the UTK. Trained by the British SAS, they were a match for any anti-terrorism unit in the world.

As the two large members of his team effortlessly carried the lifeless body of Rossa to a waiting ambulance, the crowd was focused on the now departing vice-president in the large black limousine. Those that did briefly notice saw a collapsed man being supported by two men and taken to an ambulance.

Musa turned to look at the girl. She was being led gently away by a female member of his team to another waiting ambulance some distance away. This ambulance contained two members of the bomb disposal team and would drive to the far side of the airport before they undertook their task of rendering the device harmless.

The female agent would have explained that she was now safe and that her ordeal was over. To gain her trust, she would have shown her a photo of her Malaysian friend in Vancouver. Musa was very familiar with this photograph. It was his favourite one of his son.

Musa was proud of his son studying in Vancouver, an intelligent and calm boy. The panicked phone call he had received seven days before had been most out of character.

A year previously Musa had used the intelligence resources available to him to confirm the identity of the Indonesian man he had seen, and thought he recognised, in the television coverage. It was indeed Rossa, a member of President Suharto's security detail. Musa had thought little more of this at the time. Standard surveillance of an anti-Suharto demonstration by an Indonesian Intelligence officer, he had thought. However, the revelation from his son's recent phone call that the Indonesian man had reappeared, and driven the young Indonesian girl away, and the unexplained disappearance of their friend, spelt that an operation was under way. The timing suggested this was very likely related to the upcoming APEC meeting in KL.

The son had been at pains to tell his father that the girl was not a radical in any way and that she would not be involved with anything illegal.

Given the heightened security awareness for APEC98, Musa would normally have placed identities of both Rossa and his son's friend on the immigration watch list. They could then have been picked up the instant they tried to enter Malaysia.

But this was not a normal situation. If Musa left any trace of direct knowledge of the individuals involved in the plot, and it were successful, he would be very lucky to escape without spending the rest of his life in jail. If the American Secret Service were to catch a whiff of a credible plot against the president, they might prevent him from attending. This would not be acceptable to his own government.

He had decided it was best to report the situation direct to President Mahathir, and his position as head of the key anti-terrorist police team allowed him that privilege.

Like any host head of any state, Mahathir was very focused on the success of his opportunity to shine on the world stage. He had given Musa two very clear instructions. Nothing was to interfere with the smooth running and security of APEC in KL, and this Indonesian, Mr Rossa, was either working for the Indonesian government or in a freelance capacity. Either way, as the new president of Indonesia Habibie would be present for his first APEC, the close bonds between the Muslim 'brothers' of Malaysia and Indonesia must not be strained. At least on the world stage during the APEC meeting.

Musa had understood clearly. Knowledge of the

potential plot would need to be kept to his anti-terror team and he could take whatever action he wished as long as it created no fuss.

He watched as Rossa's body was placed in the ambulance. It would be taken for an autopsy which would state that he had died of a heart attack. It would then be thoroughly embalmed, removing any trace of the cocktail of drugs used to render him unconscious and stop his heart. The body would then be flown back to Indonesia.

The Indonesian girl was walking with her minder to the second ambulance. Musa thought, and hoped for his son's sake, that the debriefing would confirm she was an unwilling participant. If she had been coerced it would likely have involved threats against her family. She would be returned to Jakarta with a warning that to speak to anyone regarding the incident could place her, and her family, in danger.

He also reflected that the backup safety net he had put in place had not been required. On leaving his meeting with President Mahathir, he had decided that the most likely scenario was an attempt on the President of the USA. If this was successful on Malaysian soil, and the Americans found out that Malaysian security had had some advance warning, the implications for his country would be extreme. At the same time, if warning the Americans resulted in the President of the USA not attending the meeting and this warning were traced back to him, the impact on him from President Mahathir would likely be extreme also.

He was well aware that the American National Security Agency's focus on listening to communications within his country would be at the highest level, given the upcoming meeting. He decided on five keywords or phrases that could be inserted into communications.

President Clinton, assassination attempt, APEC98, credible threat and, for good measure, Muslim.

All he needed to do now was to call someone and weave all of these keywords and phrases into the conversation. He decided to call his trusted second in command who he had briefed on the situation.

Using his own cellphone, he had called his colleague and used all the keywords and phrases in the conversation. He was confident that, given his position as head of the anti-terrorism police for the event, NSA would be monitoring his phone calls. The keywords would be detected by the monitoring software and result in more detailed analysis of the call. This would conclude in various US agencies undertaking a threat assessment and updating the US Secret Service regarding the risk.

He was confident that the Secret Service would not allow the president to travel to KL. At the same time, they could not question him or the Malaysian forces regarding the matter without disclosing that they were monitoring communications. They would never do this as this would compromise their own operations. So Musa should not have to answer any awkward questions either from President Mahathir or the US authorities.

While the loss of the US Vice-President on Malaysian

soil during APEC would have been quite devastating, it would be nowhere near as catastrophic as the assassination of the US President.

Musa would again call his son in Vancouver later this evening and simply tell him his friend was safe and well.

Chapter Seventeen

The four old men sat around the fireplace in the library. The heat from the fire was welcome on a cold night in Connecticut in early January. The house was one of the finest in America and the country estate was large and secluded. It was home to one of the men present, an American and native of Connecticut. Of the three guests present, two were American and one Swiss. Between the four of them they controlled 90 percent of the world's pharmaceutical industry. The combined worth of the companies they controlled could purchase any small country in the world and, also, quite a few of the medium-sized ones.

They had finished a fine dinner full of small talk and had now retired to the library, settled into their large leather chairs and, with no one else present in the room, they could now address the purpose of their meeting.

The host had filled the brandy glasses of his guests with the finest that money could buy.

'Unfortunate that the APEC meeting in Kuala Lumpur seems to have been a success,' he stated, 'other than Vice President Gore chastising President Mahathir on human rights in Malaysia, it seems to have gone well and the US push for globalisation marches on.'

There was no immediate response as each studied their brandy glass intently. It was the Swiss from Basel who broke the silence in his German-accented English. 'Our conclusion from eighteen months ago remains valid. Indeed, the APEC Meeting in Malaysia may have magnified the issue. If this march to globalisation, reducing of trade barriers and attacks on our worldwide drug patents continues, we will see a massive reduction in the value of our companies.'

There was silence once more as each studied their brandy glass and the flickering fireplace. 'Indeed,' said a second of the Americans, 'APEC99 will be held in New Zealand. Five years ago, the government of that country established a single-purchaser entity called the Pharmaceutical Management Agency, known as Pharmac. This entity purchases all of the pharmaceuticals for the entire country's extensive public health system. In the last five years the average sale price for my company's top twenty drugs sold into that country has dropped to twenty percent of what we are selling the same drugs for in the USA. We cannot allow this model to become widespread in other countries.'

After another long pause. 'So it is agreed,' said the third of the Americans in his slow Southern drawl, 'the removal of an American president with such a liberal and globalist outlook as Mr Clinton is essential to our long-term plans. If this is accomplished at an APEC event, it will have the added benefit of undermining that free trade-oriented jamboree for years to come.'

'Is it still possible?' asked the host. 'Will the authorities not be even more on their guard for the APEC meeting in Auckland, New Zealand?'

'We should ask the expert in this matter,' came the reply in the German-accented English.

With that the host rose from his chair, moved towards the fire and pressed a round button set in an ornate brass rose to one side of the fireplace. There was no noise but, within seconds, the door to the library opened and the host's personal assistant entered. She was a tall slim woman immaculately dressed and with piercing eyes.

'Would you ask our guest to join us?' said the host.

With a slight nod, the woman turned and left the room, closing the door behind her. The four men were silent once more as the door opened for a second time. The tall, pale-skinned, well-dressed gentleman entered.

'Good evening, Mr Butler,' said the host, 'do join us by the fire and would you like a brandy?'

As he moved towards an empty leather seat by the fire, Butler said, 'Good evening gentlemen, and no thank you to the brandy, sir.' He took his seat by the fire.

The host continued, 'The question has been asked if it

would be possible to re-let our contract for the APEC event to be held in Auckland next year. Does the failed attempt in Kuala Lumpur make this practical?'

Butler, in his English tones as clear as the crystal brandy glasses that each man held, said, 'My investigations of the failure of Mr Rossa at Kuala Lumpur Airport have been most illuminating. At the time of the arrival of Vice-President Gore at the airport, a man from the waiting crowd was seen being helped into an ambulance by two large men. I have since confirmed that the body of Mr Rossa has been returned to Jakarta with an explanation that he died of a heart attack. There has been no public or private discussion of an assassination attempt that I have been able to detect. It would appear that, rather than cast a shadow over their APEC event or complicate their relationship with their Indonesian neighbours, the Malaysians have been able to cover up the events that unfolded.'

'So is it your view that letting a contract for APEC99 is practical?' asked the man with the Southern drawl.

'I believe it is possible,' answered Butler.

'And how should we go about it?' asked the host.

'As you will recall, two years ago we also got a feasible proposal from a highly skilled Australian lady. I would suggest that, after confirming that there have been no major changes in her circumstances, I approach her and ascertain if she would be willing to re-engage. This would also have the advantage of not having to divulge our proposal to any new player, with the small but real risk that such widening of people with knowledge of the proposal incurs.'

The four men studied each other for a moment in complete silence. As the host looked at each in turn, there was the slightest nod of each of his guest's heads.

'Thank you, Mr Butler. Please proceed as you have outlined,' said the host.

Without any more words being spoken, Butler took his cue, rose from his seat and left the library.

Silence fell again in the room, only to be broken by the host: 'More brandy, gentlemen?'

Chapter Eighteen

It was a typical very hot day in Sydney in January of 1999. Laura Cosgrove was relaxing in one of the many cafés outside the Opera House that overlooked the Sydney Harbour Bridge. The excitement of the New Year's Eve fireworks from the bridge a few weeks before was fading into the past. They would of course be eclipsed by the show that would be put on for the millennium celebrations at the end of the year. Laura was enjoying her latte in the shade. She was just back from two months acting as a bodyguard for a female member of the Saudi royal family – a very boring but extremely lucrative engagement. Just another rich 'airhead' born into extreme wealth. She reflected that at least the Sydney heat in the height of summer was preferable to her experience of the dry heat in Riyadh.

She spotted the figure moving towards her from about sixty metres away. No one would have noticed that she had spotted him. There was no turn of her head or change in facial expression. It was simply that a lifetime of training dictated that she choose a table where no one could come up behind her and she could observe anyone approaching the café.

She continued to appear to look at her newspaper while observing the man approach. He held a steady walking pace and both of his hands were in plain sight and empty. No threat.

As he arrived at her table, she turned her head. In his perfect English accent, he said. 'Well good day, Laura, how delightful to bump into you. May I join you for coffee?' Laura responded with a welcoming smile. Mr Butler returned the smile and gave a slight bow.

'So nice to see you again,' said Laura. 'However, I thought it would be tea for you,' as she gestured for him to take a seat opposite her.

'So sorry to ruin a perfectly good stereotype, but I actually prefer coffee.'

The waitress approached and Butler ordered his trim latte. In his conversational style, Butler enquired, 'And how was Saudi Arabia. Not too arduous I hope?'

'It was an uneventful contract which in my line of work means it was a success.'

'Speaking of contracts, the one we discussed last year has resurfaced. It would be the same terms and arrangements, only you would be located in Auckland, New Zealand.'

Laura was well aware of where APEC99 would be

held. She had followed with interest the press coverage of the meeting in Kuala Lumpur. She had noted the absence of any major incident and, while her mind had turned over a number of scenarios as to why that might be the case, she had not considered that she would see Butler again.

'Are you interested?' he asked.

'This is most interesting,' said Laura. Each of them held a casual pose and slight smile. To any observer who had seen Butler arrive, they were simply two acquaintances having a coffee and a casual chat.

In complete contrast to her expression, Laura's thoughts were racing. If she undertook this contract, it would be the last she would ever need to do. After another year of acting as bodyguard for rich people, she knew more than ever that she wanted to be a rich person.

'May I ask,' enquired Laura, 'the previous contract in this matter, I assume you let the contract? Has it left any heightened awareness that I should be aware of?'

'The contract was let but the target of the proposed services was never aware that the contract was in place.'

Laura thought for a moment and took a long sip of her latte. That she was being approached again showed an increased eagerness on the part of Butler's employers to complete the contract. She decided to leverage that. It was a risk, but she had been trained to take calculated risks. She also estimated that Butler had more discretion on the letting of the contract than he professed. She decided to test that.

'It is my view that the risk has increased, and I would

like to make three alterations to my original proposal to you.'

'Go ahead,' said Butler.

'The cost will be 20 million US dollars and there is to be a non-refundable twenty percent down-payment.'

Laura paused and took another sip of coffee.

'And the third variation?' asked Butler.

'You need to accept my proposal within the next twenty-four hours.'

It was Butler's turn to take a long drink of coffee, as the sun shone and the tourists passed by. He returned his cup to its saucer. 'Is the Cayman Islands bank account number in your proposal from last year still your chosen account?'

'Yes, it is.'

'Then if your terms are acceptable, the four million US dollars initial payment will be deposited in your account within twenty-four hours. If your terms are not acceptable, there will be no deposit.'

Butler continued. 'It has been a pleasure meeting with you, Ms Cosgrove, but regardless of the acceptability of your proposal or not I think it is unlikely we will meet again. May I wish you a long and prosperous life.'

Not for the first time a compliment from Mr Butler, delivered in a most gentlemanly fashion, sent a slight chill down Laura's spine.

Butler rose from the table, turned and ambled back in the direction he had come.

When Laura checked her Cayman Islands bank

account the following day the balance showed as
US$4,000,000.

The next step for her was to arrange to meet with two old friends. She knew her life would never be the same again.

Chapter Nineteen

At about the time of Laura's meeting in Sydney, over a thousand miles away across the Tasman Sea, the now two-weekly meeting of the APEC security team was taking place.

The meeting was chaired by Superintendent Charles Bolt as the operation commander and overall head of security for APEC99.

It was the superintendent's habit to go around the table and ask each member for a brief update on progress and any potential issues they wished to raise.

Joe had given a PowerPoint presentation on the thirteen key technology projects that would be in place for the event. While there were no issues with any of them, he had tried to avoid the phrase 'on time and on budget'. This had become a well-mistrusted phrase in relation to public sector technology projects in New Zealand. It was the equivalent to a football team manager in the English

League receiving a vote of confidence from the club's board. The sack was invariably imminent.

Brad's update included one of the most sensitive topics: the ability of foreign security personnel to carry firearms on New Zealand soil. Brad explained that each of the delegations might have a requirement, but chief among them would be the US Secret Service. They had the right to prevent the president from travelling anywhere domestically or overseas if they felt it was unsafe. They had indicated that the president travelling to New Zealand would not happen if they were not allowed to carry firearms.

This, of course, had to be balanced with the fact that New Zealanders are not accustomed to seeing, nor want to see, their police officers armed, other than in international airports where it is required by international convention. The idea, being magnified by media, of a hundred American Secret Service agents running around waving guns did not appeal to either police or politicians. While certain covert accommodations may have been made in the past, APEC was far too high profile for this approach to work in this instance.

Brad's approach had been to try to resolve the issue with the US Secret Service. If he found a solution for them, hopefully this approach could be used for all other delegations.

Contrary to the picture painted in many Hollywood action movies, members of the FBI or US Secret Service have no authority to carry firearms in overseas countries.

Nor would they allow an overseas law enforcement officer to carry a firearm in the US.

The completely novel approach taken by Brad was for the Commissioner of Police to grant temporary constable status to a limited number of the security detail of any delegation that requested it, subject to that request being reasonable in the eyes of the Police Commissioner. The delegation would then be able to log a limited number of firearms into the country at the start of the event. The serial number of each firearm would be recorded, and the firearm would be logged back out of the country at the conclusion of the visit.

The 'in principle' discussions with the US Secret Service had suggested they would accept thirty-two agents as temporary constables authorised to carry a firearm. Eight firearms would be registered for them to share.

'Of course,' said Brad, 'a drawback is that I am sure that it is not beyond the ability of the Secret Service to have many firearms manufactured with the same serial number. They would then be able to register eight on arrival and bring another fifty of each with the same serial number. However, this approach appears to be the only way to solve the problem with the US Secret Service and ensure that the president travels to New Zealand. It will, of course, require legislation to be passed through Parliament to give the police commissioner this authority.' He rested his gaze on Sir Reggie.

'Thank you,' said Sir Reggie. 'May I compliment you on a most creative solution. I will inform the prime minister of this approach that will place a very small number of firearms in the hands of a small number of very highly trained personal protection officers for some delegations. If it meets her approval, I am sure the legislation can progress through Parliament with urgency.'

There was no way that now, or at any time, Sir Reggie would be commenting on Brad's speculation regarding multiple firearms with the same serial number.

It was now Clive's turn to update the team regarding military issues. The key issue for Clive was the request from police to provide several hundred soldiers to provide boundary security for the APEC leaders' meeting to be held in the museum building in the Auckland Domain. The fencing around the park would be several kilometres in length. It was likely to be a magnet for most protests – and preventing protesters from getting over the barriers was essential.

The only problem, as in most democracies, is that police do not like the military providing crowd control and the military do not like to provide crowd control. Soldiers are not typically trained to deal with taunting aggressive individuals in a tolerant and respectful manner. They are trained to kill people.

However, police simply did not have the numbers to provide a man or woman every two metres around several kilometres of fencing. So, extensive crowd control training for the soldiers and police supervision would have to suffice.

This leader's meeting venue would be the equivalent

of the University of British Columbia meeting in Vancouver. Everyone in the room had witnessed that debacle first hand and it could not be allowed to happen in New Zealand.

Tom Shape was then asked if he had an update. His updates had been the same at every meeting so far and no one in the room imagined that this would change in the future. The only alteration was the phrase that he used to describe 'I have no update'. Today's expression, delivered with the customary smile, was 'Everything is going tickety-boo'. Not surprisingly, members of the intelligence services are not natural sharers of information.

Charles Bolt turned to Jennifer and said with a smile, 'Did you want to expand on Tom's report of the SIS position at all?'

'No, I think that covers it completely,' said Jennifer.

Charles, still smiling, turned to Sir Reggie, who was the last to deliver his update.

'Well, gentlemen and lady, I come bearing thanks from Prime Minister Shipley for the extremely important work you have done so far in planning for APEC99.'

At this point, Brad leaned over to Joe and said in his ear, 'Here it comes.'

Sir Reggie pretended not to notice and continued, 'Given the opportunity that APEC99 presents to showcase the best that New Zealand has to offer, the prime minister has decided to extend state visit invitations to the President of the United States of America, Bill Clinton, the President of China, Jiang Zemin and the

President of South Korea, Kim Dae-jung. The itineraries for the three state visits are currently under active discussion. Each is likely to be two or three days long, immediately following the close of the APEC leaders' meeting.

There was no audible sigh in the room, but the body language of the APEC team spoke volumes. APEC would already be putting the greatest ever strain on the police's manpower. To extend this with three state visits on the tail of the APEC event would add to this burden on resources considerably.

It was Charles Bolt, with his consummate political skills – not a charge often levelled at many senior police officers – who broke the silence.

'Well, if that is what Prime Minister Shipley wants, then of course we will facilitate it. Do you have any initial indications of likely events and locations during the visits?'

Sir Reggie pondered for a moment. 'Each will likely involve a state dinner and an official meeting with the Governor General, as the Queen's representative, probably lunch at his official residence. Oh, and President Clinton has expressed an interest in a game of golf.'

Brad was about to say something when he looked at Charles. He immediately stopped when he recognised the look he got back. It was 'leave this to me'. There would be no negative comments about political decisions, at least not in front of Sir Reggie.

Chapter Twenty

The view over Auckland's Viaduct Harbour from the restaurant verandah was spectacular. It was a very warm January summer's evening and the moonlight was dancing on the gently swaying masts of the large yachts.

The Viaduct had been quite a rundown area of Auckland. It was, however, going through a major development ahead of the defence of the America's Cup yacht races in 2000. New Zealand's first win in one of the world's oldest sporting events in 1995 in San Diego had galvanised and enthralled the nation. It would also provide a whole new set of novel water-based issues for New Zealand police.

'This is a very romantic setting you have brought me to, Mr Edwards,' said Jennifer.

'I very much hope so,' responded Joe, as the waiter interrupted them with the main course.

It had been three months since the afternoon in The Mines hotel in Kuala Lumpur. They had only managed to meet a few times since. But their feelings for each other were growing.

They ate their fish and settled back to finish the last of a delightful bottle of New Zealand Sauvignon Blanc.

'You know, you are an even more mysterious woman in the moonlight,' said Joe with a smile. 'I don't even have your mobile phone number and you never answer your work number. It always goes to voicemail. I don't think you even have a desk. Do you actually have a mobile phone number?'

'That's classified,' said Jennifer with a smile.

'You like that, don't you? To me, it makes you even more mysterious.'

Jennifer looked at Joe. 'I like that you know what I do for a living. You know that I spend a lot of my time pretending to be someone else and with you I don't have to. Thank you for not asking questions when I say I cannot meet you. It is not because I don't want to.'

'I know,' said Joe, 'but it is nice to hear you say it. I understand that there will always be a lot of your life you cannot share with me.' Deciding this was getting a bit serious, Joe continued, 'Oh, and by the way, I would just like to say that you get major style points for never using the cliché "I could tell you but then I would have to kill you". Which in your case you probably could.'

Jennifer pulled a serious face and said, 'Almost instantly with this blunt fish knife.'

'Ouch,' said Joe.

They looked at each other as they took a sip of cool wine and the warm wind from the South Pacific caressed them.

The moment was interrupted by the sound of a mobile phone ringing. Joe looked around to see who it was and, as he looked back, he saw Jennifer take a phone from her jacket pocket. She did have a mobile phone.

As Jennifer moved the phone to her ear, she looked Joe straight in the eyes and said, 'Jenny here.' She then rose from her seat and moved to the far end of the verandah where her conversation could not be overheard.

After a few minutes she returned to the table, picked up her wine and took a sip.

Jennifer found the need to share a secret with Joe.

'I use the name Jenny when I am working undercover. You see, it is important when you are working under an assumed name that when someone says your name you respond instantly. It does not matter how tired or distracted you might be. If you do not respond instantly it might raise suspicions that you are not who you say you are. Unfortunately, I don't like the name Jenny but...'

'Then I will never call you by that name.' Joe recognised that Jennifer had just shared something else with him. She could have moved to the end of the verandah before taking the call. She had chosen not to.

She smiled at him as she saw the recognition on his face.

'Would you like to come back to my apartment for coffee?' asked Joe.

'I don't drink coffee this late in the evening,' said an impish Jennifer.

'That's okay,' said Joe, 'I don't think I have any.'

Chapter Twenty-One

Laura settled in to her business-class seat for the three-and-a-half-hour flight back from Auckland to Sydney. She had flown into Auckland the day before to meet with her friend. The night had been a sweet mix of business and pleasure. Her body felt satisfied and her mind focused. She declined the glass of champagne offered by the flight steward and settled for a glass of orange juice.

The relationship with her New Zealand friend had been simmering on and off for over ten years. Their chosen professions had meant lengthy periods when they could not meet. She had taken him into her full confidence the night before. They both knew well the high stakes involved with her plan. In a few months their life together would change radically. The only question would be if this would be for better or worse. It was up to her to make sure it was the former.

It had been two weeks since her meeting with Mr Butler and she had been considering a number of options. The discussion the previous night had brought one of those to the front of her mind. As she drank her orange juice, solutions to key elements of the plan seemed to fall into place.

She would need to enter and leave New Zealand for APEC99 on a false identity and rent the vehicle she wanted on another false identity. In the relatively recent past, this would have simply involved a fake passport. Present it to an overworked and bored immigration officer and she would be fine. However, she had also learnt the previous evening that not only would New Zealand immigration officers be making use of an enhanced computer database to check all passports arriving for the event but the arrival details of all individuals were being shared with US Intelligence agencies for a period of at least three months before the event started.

She was going to need something special by the way of a passport. She was not quite sure what, but she was sure that a man she had dealt with before in Sydney would.

The following day Laura entered the run-down building on the edge of Sydney's city centre. Kings Cross had for decades been the city's foremost red-light area. Populated with bars, nightclubs and massage parlours, the area had something for all tastes.

As Laura entered the building, she noted that it catered for all three major pastimes. There was a nightclub in the basement, a bar on the ground floor and several massage parlours on the first and second floors – a virtual 'one-stop shop'. Her contact had chosen his premises well. The movement of people twenty-four hours a day meant that no one took any real notice of anyone.

She made her way to the third and top floor. At the end of the corridor, she was faced with a very sturdy steel door. There was a bell push to one side and a video camera above. This was not Laura's first visit to this 'office' and she knew the routine. She pressed the bell push and looked up at the video camera. After a minute, a diminutive man with a thin face opened the door.

'Good day, nice to see you again. It must have been two years or so.'

'And you also.' In their previous two meetings, neither had offered or asked for a real name.

'Do come in.' The man closed the door behind Laura, which made a decidedly heavy thud.

They moved through the dimly lit reception area to his main office. There was no one else around. Laura had never actually seen anyone else in the office.

The man moved behind a large antique desk and, as he lowered himself into a leather office chair, he waved for Laura to take a seat opposite.

'And how may I assist?' said the master forger.

'I have a special set of circumstances and seek your advice on resolving them.'

'Please continue,' said the man as he picked up his pen and hovered it over a pad of writing paper.

'I require two fake identities together with a passport and driver's licence for each. The first passport and driver's licence will only be used for the purchase of local services. They will not be used for entry to a country, so straightforward Australian forgeries will suffice.'

'And what name would you like?' asked the forger.

'Christine Stephenson.'

'That will not be a problem.'

'The second passport may be more problematic. I require a passport and matching driver's licence, again for myself. There will be a single entry into a country and a single exit. The time spent in the country will be about two weeks. Both the passport and driver's licence will be used only for this period. The immigration authorities will be on a heightened state of alert for all arrivals and will have access to their national crime fighting and intelligence databases as well as the full cooperation of a number of overseas intelligence agencies and their databases.'

Laura paused. The man looked up from his note taking and asked, 'The name of the country to be visited and the nationality of the passport?'

'The country will be New Zealand and my nationality is to be Australian.'

'A wise choice of nationality if I may say. Always best to choose a country with which you have intimate knowledge. A hesitant answer to an immigration officer regarding a question on a trivial matter from your chosen country, such as a local landmark, can bring about unwanted attention.'

The man smiled and continued. 'May I assume that the entry period into the country will be September this year?'

They studied each other for a moment.

'You follow world events,' said Laura.

'I try to keep up to date.'

Another moment passed as they regarded each other again.

'The level of passport scrutiny will be extreme,' said the forger. 'I would not recommend a forged passport, in this instance. Although I can produce a near-flawless document, the absence of a usage history or corroborating database information, driving licence record, tax record, even a minor criminal conviction, is likely to raise a red flag.

'It is going to get increasingly difficult to use a forged passport. The days of an immigration officer simply looking at a passport are coming to an end. The passport will be checked against multiple databases, and there are even future moves being suggested to embed fingerprints and other biometric data on a computer chip within the passport.'

After a pause the forger said, 'I think we need a clean skin.'

'Clean skin?' said Laura. 'I am not familiar with the term.'

'A clean skin is a passport and driver's licence of a real person. We "borrow" them for the period that is required. The first step is to identify someone with features suitably similar to your own.'

'Go on,' said Laura.

'We do not require an exact match. A facial resemblance and approximately the same height, age and ethnic background will suffice. Hair colour is easily dealt with.'

'How do we prevent this person from noticing that we have borrowed their passport?' asked Laura.

'There are two main approaches. The first if the owner of the passport is willing is a financial inducement to borrow the passport for a period of time. The second option if the owner of the passport is not cooperative is to obtain the passport and ensure that the owner does not report it lost or stolen for the period you require it.'

Laura contemplated the forger for a few moments. There were pros and cons to either approach. 'And the next steps?' said Laura.

'I can have a portfolio of photographs and personal details of likely candidates for you in three days.'

'You have access to the Australian passport database?' asked Laura.

The forger merely looked at her and smiled. She would have been a little concerned regarding his professionalism if he had answered.

'And the fee?' asked Laura.

'$10,000 for the forged passport and driver's licence in

the name of Christine Stephenson. The portfolio of potential candidates will be $25,000. A further $25,000 will be due if you choose to progress with one of the candidates.' After a brief pause, he continued, 'There will, of course, be further charges should you wish to contract any additional services with regard to obtaining the passport and neutralising the risk of discovery.'

'That sounds expensive for merely identifying the clean skin passport.'

'Yes,' said the forger. 'You will appreciate that, while the forged passport is produced in-house, for the clean skin I have to make certain expense payments.'

'Bribes,' said Laura.

The forger just smiled again.

She smiled back and said, 'That fee is acceptable then. What do you require from me now?'

'I will need the personal details for Ms Christine Stephenson and a selection of passport-sized photographs.'

Laura opened her bag and extracted a brown envelope and handed it to the forger. He opened it and studied the contents. It contained a sheet of paper with date and place of birth and other details for Christine Stephenson and four passport-sized photographs of Laura in which she is wearing a blonde wig.

The forger scanned the personal details and then studied the photographs. 'It is always a delight to deal with a true professional. This is the best of the photographs for the passport, and I will use this slightly different one for the driver's licence.'

'Agreed,' said Laura, 'and when can they be ready?'

'If you return in three days, I will have the Stephenson passport and driver's licence ready. I will also have a portfolio of candidates for the "clean skin" identity for you to review.'

With that the meeting was over and the master forger escorted Laura from the offices.

Chapter Twenty-Two

Laura had arranged to see her old friend Captain Alex Conrad the following day. It had been over a year since she had spoken to him when she had been working on the original proposal for the APEC meeting in Kuala Lumpur. She had not said anything explicit to him, but the understanding was there. After twenty-five years as a pilot in the Royal Australian Air Force he was nearing the end of his career. Considered one of their finest pilots, he had spent the last eleven years attached to the Australian SAS as their chief pilot. He was the go-to pilot to get them into and, more importantly, out of any of their deployments anywhere in the world.

Alex knew he was coming to the end of his military career and the prospect of retiring on a meagre pension appealed to him even less than the idea of becoming a 'bus driver' on some commercial airline flying back and forward on the same route. He had known too much excitement and danger in his career for that to interest him.

When Laura had called, Alex had been keen to catch up. She had been relieved that he was in Australia and pleased when he suggested the following day. Laura had decided the location, Sydney Zoo.

Sydney's Taronga Zoo is located on a hillside across the harbour from downtown Sydney. It can be reached by ferry or road and is a very popular attraction with both locals and tourists. If you position yourself, just right, on the path above the giraffe enclosure, it is possible to take a photo of the giraffes with the Sydney Opera House and harbour bridge in the background. If the giraffes had been able to charge a dollar for every one of those photos taken, they could have bought the zoo outright, several times over.

Having met at the entrance and exchanged some small talk, Laura and Alex had settled on a very quiet bench overlooking some amorous chimpanzees.

'Tell me about Stinger missiles,' said Laura matter-of-factly.

Alex paused and looked at her for a moment. He was interested to see where this was going. He would play along.

'Stinger missiles are an American-made MANPAD, Man Portable Air Defence System. They consist of a launcher unit and missile. The Stinger entered service in 1981. It is five feet long and, together, the missile and launcher weigh 15.2 kg. The missile can be fired by a single person. There are variants but the most common has a sophisticated infrared homing system designed to lock onto the heat exhaust of a fixed-wing plane or helicopter.

'It has a range of about 15,000 feet, depending on the model, a speed of Mach 2.4 and a three-kilo high-explosive fragmentation warhead. Enough explosive power to take out any small to medium aircraft.'

Alex stopped at that point and just looked at Laura.

'Tell me about Stingers in Afghanistan.'

Alex studied her once more. They were still on their own with only the chimps for company.

'When the Soviet Union invaded Afghanistan in 1979, they owned the sky. In particular their armoured-attack helicopter called the Hind. These helicopters were impervious to machine-gun fire from all but the heaviest guns. In the rugged terrain covering most of the country, they tilted the war in favour of the Soviets. An American Congressman called Charlie Wilson was persuaded to do something about this. He managed to obtain funds for the CIA to supply the Afghan freedom fighters, the Mujahideen, with Stinger missiles. The first Stinger success was a Russian Hind helicopter downed in September 1986. Accurate total numbers of Soviet aircraft downed in the conflict are difficult to get to but probably amount to several hundred. The result was that the Soviets lost control of the air and, within two years, they had lost the war and were pulling out of Afghanistan.

Most analysts credit the Stinger as changing the course of the war.'

'How many Stingers did the Americans supply?' asked Laura.

'The official CIA number was 500 but more realistic estimates indicate up to 2000. The Soviets finally completed their pull-out from Afghanistan in 1989, ten years ago. The Americans then became very concerned about all the unused Stingers lying around in the hands of a local Muslim irregular army. The CIA was allocated about $55 million to buy them back. Not much news on how many they got back but the word among the Special Forces family is that about 600 remained unaccounted for, and since then they have been turning up in all sorts of countries including Qatar, Iran and North Korea. Two years ago and eight years after the end of the Afghan–Russian conflict, the Tamil Tigers of Eelam used one to shoot down a Sri Lankan government helicopter. By chance, but rather fittingly, it was a Hind attack helicopter supplied to the Sri Lankans by Russia.'

'The monkeys are very entertaining,' said Laura in an elevated voice as two young parents pushing a baby in a buggy went past. Alex picked up the cue and a zoo conversation about monkeys progressed until the couple were out of earshot.

'So why don't you ask me the question you got me here to ask?' said Alex.

'Before we get to that, I have two other questions,' said Laura evasively. 'Will you be flying the Australian SAS contingent and their tons of equipment to APEC in Auckland in September? I assume they will be providing security for Prime Minister Howard and helping out their overstretched New Zealand counterparts with the event. And, secondly, are you still flying in and out of Afghanistan with the Australian Special Forces deployed there at the moment?'

'Yes, to both,' said Alex. 'So ask me what you really want to know.' A moment passed before Laura responded.

'I want you to deliver a fully functional Stinger missile to me in Auckland.'

Alex had not been surprised by the request, but the location of the delivery had given him pause for thought. He finally said, 'I won't insult you by asking you to tell me who the target is. However, I intend to retire in Australia. Is the primary target an Australian?'

'No, the person is not,' Laura answered firmly.

'Then the answer is yes... for the right price.'

Laura levelled her gaze at Alex. 'Before you answer my next questions I need you to be deadly certain.' She emphasised the word 'deadly'. 'As you might expect, the people I work for are very serious and very powerful. If you agree to this and do not deliver to me a fully functioning Stinger, you will not be retiring anywhere. I emphasise that the missile must be fully functioning. I hear that the batteries can be a problem after four or five years. If there are any slip-ups, then neither you nor I will survive and nor may our closest friends and family.'

Alex returned her gaze. He was not surprised that she

knew of the battery problems with the Stingers. In fact, he would have been surprised if she were not aware of everything he had told her. Her questions regarding the Stingers and Afghanistan had simply been a preamble to the purpose of the meeting.

Alex knew from conversations during downtime in Afghanistan between flights that Stingers were available for the right price. The last he had heard, the going rate was US$250,000. They had been cheaper a few years previously but stocks must be dwindling. He also suspected that Laura would know the going price as well.

He decided that the time for prevaricating was over. Now it was down to business. 'Half a million US dollars up front to buy the missile and one million US dollars to get it out of Afghanistan and into Auckland,' he stated.

'The price of postage these days,' sighed Laura. 'Agreed. I assume you want the 500,000 in cash?'

'Indeed.'

'When we meet in Auckland, I will check the delivery. I will then make a phone call and the US one-million-dollar balance will be immediately deposited in the bank of your choice. You will be able to confirm this before I leave with the package.'

'I would expect nothing less,' said Alex.

'I will also want an automatic pistol, about fifty rounds of ammunition and a small incendiary explosive with a tilt-timer detonator,' said Laura.

'I will throw them in free,' said Alex with a smile. 'When can I expect to take delivery of the half million?'

'Come with me to the carpark now. I have it in a briefcase in the boot of my car.'

Laura had of course chosen to drive to the zoo rather than take the ferry. Alex had spent many years now working with elite individuals whose planning was often the difference between life and death. That Laura had the exact down-payment for the missile with her did not surprise him. For the second time in a week, one of her specialised contacts experienced satisfaction that he was dealing with a professional.

They both rose from the seat, leaving the chimps to their endless cavorting, and strolled casually towards the carpark.

Chapter Twenty-Three

Laura returned to the forger's office three days after her recent visit. She sat in the chair opposite his desk.

'The passport and driver's licence for Christine Stephenson,' he said as he handed them to Laura. She studied them carefully, making sure that the personal details on each matched.

'They look fine,' she said.

He then handed her six sheets of paper. Each sheet contained a photograph of a woman who looked very similar to Laura. The pages also detailed physical characteristics, address and some background information on marital status and profession.

Three of the identified women were married. Laura placed these pages on the forger's desk and concentrated on the three single women. A single woman might be a better fit for what Laura had in mind.

'This one looks promising,' said Laura.

The forger inspected the photograph and then looked at Laura.

'Yes, definitely promising. Her passport is valid for another four years and was last used just two months ago. A holiday trip to Bali it looks like. The colour of the eyes and the hair colour are different to yours. Also, she wears glasses. This is an advantage as I am sure you are aware. It would make any attempt to map this face to yours after your use of the passport more difficult.'

'Are you expecting that the authorities will search for and find this person after your exercise is complete?'

'It is very likely,' said Laura.

'So a bribe or any other action that might leave a trail for the authorities to follow back to you is not practical?'

The forger continued. 'The scenario is that we need to acquire her passport. She must not report it lost or stolen for the period you require it, and she must not try to travel overseas during this period either. Also, she must not die, as the passport would be cancelled. Would you require some contracted assistance in obtaining the passport?'

'No, thank you,' said Laura. 'I will obtain it myself.'

'Then, if I can be of no further assistance, so at this point there is just the matter of my fee.'

Laura handed the man an envelope containing the $60,000. 'Ten thousand for the forged passport and driver's licence and fifty thousand for the clean skin identity as agreed.'

The forger took the envelope and quickly flicked

through the large bundle of bills it contained. Satisfied that the payment was in order, he said, 'A pleasure doing business with you once more. If there are no further matters, may I show you out?'

Laura nodded and they both rose from their chairs.

Chapter Twenty-Four

I t is a three-hour drive from Auckland to Ruffins Bay on the Coromandel Peninsula. The journey starts on a four-lane motorway and finishes on a narrow one-lane rough track past a signpost saying Private Road.

The geography for the meeting had been well chosen by the targets of the operation. The drive finished with a three-kilometre run down a 'No exit' road, Wyuna Bay Road, which ran along a narrow peninsula to the picturesque Wyuna Bay. There was then a further 500 metres down the private Ruffins Bay Road. This amounted to three and a half kilometres of one road in and the same road out from the house.

As Jennifer drove down the winding peninsula, she passed a collection of houses. They seemed to cascade down to the water's edge. The view would have been spectacular, but it was nearly midnight and was a black March night with no moon.

Tom was located in a large old motorhome parked by the Coromandel town pier. The location gave him, the SIS technical officer and the third person in the van a line of sight across the calm water of the Coromandel Harbour to Ruffins Bay on the opposite side.

The van was filled with a green glow from the night-vision monitor displaying the view from across the harbour. The heavily tinted windows were covered in tight-fitting blackout curtains. No light would escape the van to attract any curious onlooker.

'I still do not like this,' said Tom. His two colleagues in the van said nothing. They had heard this comment a dozen times so far this evening and knew there was no response they could give that would make Tom like it any more.

There had been no option to have a close-support team follow Jennifer to the meeting. They would be spotted immediately. That there would be one or more lookouts stationed on the single road to the picturesque bay was a certainty. They had also decided that it would be too dangerous to have Jennifer wired with communications. It was very likely that she would be scanned for listening devices before she entered the house. If one were found, it was unlikely she would make it out of the picturesque holiday location alive.

They did have a communications link into the car. This link would only work if the unobtrusive standard car radio had the pre-set numbers 2 and 4 both depressed together. Tom flicked the switch in front of him in the motorhome and spoke into the microphone.

'Confirm all is okay.'

In the car a smile came on Jennifer's face. 'Thanks, Dad, I am still all excited for my first date.'

There was only ten years' difference in their ages, but Tom had always been a mentor to Jennifer.

Tom allowed himself a slight grin. 'Well, if anybody's hands go where they are not supposed to, I want you straight home from that party, Jenny.'

'Understood,' came the response. The Jenny sign-off was Tom's way of noting that it was now 'game-on' time.

'I am approaching the venue and going off comms.' With that 'Jenny' selected pre-set channel 1 on the radio and the comms went silent.

On the green screen in the motorhome, the three operatives watched as the car moved slowly along the last of the single-track road and came to a stop in front of the largest of the dozen or so houses that clung to the shoreline in the small Ruffins Bay.

Jenny parked the car in front of the house. As she got out a very large man, Polynesian she thought, came towards her from the shadows. He moved very quietly for someone well over two metres tall and 125 kilograms, she thought.

'Good evening, miss,' he said as he arrived alongside her. 'May I ask your name?' he enquired almost casually.

'Jenny.'

'May I ask that you turn off your mobile phone and give it to me please?

Jenny took out her mobile, turned it off and handed it to him.

He removed a small device from his pocket and waved it over the phone. Satisfied that the phone was not transmitting, he moved to the car and waved the device over the car. The device continued to make a low hum and gave no indication that the car was transmitting, which, of course, it was not.

He then turned his attention back to Jenny.

'I just need to wave this wand over you and pat you down. Would you put your arms out, please?'

Jennifer did as she was asked, and the large man moved the device over her whole body. He then placed the device back in his jacket and expertly moved his hands all over Jenny's body in search of weapons.

As he checked up the top of her legs and crotch, Jennifer had two thoughts. One was this man had been well-trained; this was a proper pat down, nothing gratuitous about it. The second thought that made her smile slightly was 'I hope my dad is not watching this.'

He was.

As the large man completed his work, he said, 'Thank you, Miss Jenny. Please go into the house.'

As Jennifer approached the front door of the beach house, it was opened by a man not much smaller than the one outside. This person, however, had a large facial tattoo, and not one of the cultural tattoos favoured by some

Maori and Polynesians. This one undeniably signified membership of a motorcycle gang. He stood back from the doorway and signalled her to enter.

'Step one completed,' said the third man in the motorhome with Tom, in his broad New York accent.

Chuck Smith, Tom thought, was a very poor alias to choose for a senior CIA agent.

It had been only two weeks since Chuck had come to New Zealand to meet with the director of the SIS and Tom. The meeting had taken place in a nondescript house in a quiet suburb of Wellington. The CIA had become aware, no explanation given or asked, that a person of interest known as the 'Exporter', was planning a trip to New Zealand. The Exporter was known to the CIA as an international arms trafficker. He would arrange delivery of firearms to any location in the world. The only country in the world he would not deliver arms to was the US. When arms were so plentiful and cheap, there was no market for his services. But, more importantly, this was where he worked and lived. Not having so much as a speeding ticket, he would give local law enforcement no reason to be interested in him.

The situation as Chuck explained was very 'delicate'. The CIA by law is not allowed to conduct investigations on US soil. But they could not avoid investigating when a sophisticated arms dealer was visiting a country just ahead of the long-publicised arrival of the US President.

If it were to become known that the CIA was assisting a foreign government, even a friendly one like New

Zealand, to investigate a US citizen, questions would be asked. The CIA would prefer not to have to answer questions from some congressional oversight committee as to whether they had been surveying a US citizen on US soil.

For this reason, the request from the CIA was for this to be a discreet 'off the books' operation. If the Exporter's activity in New Zealand turned out to be merely criminal and not related to the forthcoming APEC meeting, the CIA's preference would be for a quiet conclusion. The New Zealand Police were not to be involved. The ability of the SIS to turn a blind eye to criminal activity if they thought it was in the national interest was not an option open to a sworn New Zealand police officer.

An intelligence-gathering operation had been agreed upon. It quickly became apparent that the Exporter was coming to New Zealand to meet the head of the largest motorcycle gang.

At that point, back in the house, 'Please sit down' came the instruction to Jenny from the man across the table.

The room was dimly lit but Jenny recognised him. He was known as 'Chain' and was the head of the largest and most violent of the New Zealand gangs. His nickname had derived from his preference for using a motorcycle chain as a weapon in 'altercations' during his early years in the gang.

As Jennifer sat in the chair opposite Chain, she noticed a second man sitting in an armchair in the corner.

The space he had chosen placed him in the darkest part of the dimly lit room. But from all of the surveillance photos that she had reviewed, she could just make out that it was the Exporter.

Like any SIS officer at any point in time, Jennifer would be cultivating a number of 'legends' for Jenny to use. They were more than just aliases for her. Each of them was a carefully crafted individual that had histories, health records, tax numbers and records, passports, credit cards and employee records at selected employers. They would also have prior addresses where, if asked, a person at the address would state that they had lived there at some time.

It was Jenny Simpson who now sat in the room being carefully watched by the two men. Miss Simpson was a Customs officer. She had been an average employee of New Zealand Customs for two years now. Most things were average about Jenny Simpson. The one thing that was out of the ordinary and, which Miss Simpson kept from her employers and work colleagues, was her gambling habits. She preferred horse racing but really was quite happy to gamble on most things. A run of bad luck on slow horses meant that she was now in debt to a South Auckland bookmaker. This debt was large and, unfortunately, with the punitive interest rate attached, was growing fast. The bookie was well known in organised crime circles. Also known, and feared, was that he used the country's largest and most vicious motorcycle gang to perform his debt-collection tasks.

The bookie had his own contact in the Inland Revenue Department, someone who was working off a debt that would never actually be fully repaid. This IRD contact was very useful in checking on individuals who were running up large debts and giving an indication if they were going to be able to repay them. The information he received from his IRD mole led him to two conclusions: how little a new Customs officer paid in tax on their very meagre salary; and that Miss Simpson might be worth more than the simple debt she owed.

Having consulted with the head of his 'debt collection agency', the bookie had recently, rather forcefully, suggested to Jenny Simpson that she had two options: pay back the debt instantly, or meet with his chief debt collector who was interested in working something out with her. As Jenny did not have the means to pay off the debt, she had been forced to attend the meeting.

'Well, Jenny, I understand you have had a run of bad luck on the horses.' The words came easily from Chain.

'I have,' said Jenny in an attempted defiant tone that was less convincing due to the slight shake in her voice.

'You have nothing to worry about this evening. You are free to leave at any time. If you choose to leave, then the gentleman you met at the door will be in touch with you in the next day or so to... discuss your debt-repayment schedule. The fact that you are here, however, would seem to suggest you may be open to an alternative suggestion.'

Jenny paused for a moment. 'What do you have in mind?'

'We have a requirement to urgently import a number of items. We would like you to... shall we say... chaperone those items through the Customs process.'

Jennifer was surprised by the subtlety in Chain's language as she had seen photos of the beatings he had dealt to those who did not follow his orders. But at the same time, it took more than brute violence to remain the head of a large criminal organisation as he did.

'What would the items be?' asked Jenny.

'The initial delivery will be 100 pistols. Following that a mixture of pistols and drugs,' Chain said as he stared intently at Jenny. She noticed that the man in the corner continued his impersonation of a disinterested observer.

The openness of his statement surprised Jennifer. He had effortlessly moved from subtlety to an open challenge for her to respond. But something did not add up. While this might be a big issue for a New Zealand motorcycle gang, it was far too small for the Exporter to get involved in, let alone put in a personal appearance at such a meeting.

'There will also be some more complicated undertakings for you. Certain shipments will arrive into New Zealand which will be documented as high-value machine parts. They will, in fact, be firearms. While they remain in the Customs area, and before they are inspected, you will alter the documentation and arrange for them to be exported to a third country.'

After a long pause, Jenny said, 'I will need time to think this over.'

'Of course,' said Chain, dripping with insincerity. He glared at Jenny and then continued loudly, 'There, that should be long enough time. Give me your answer now.'

'What are the terms?'

'Your debt will be wiped and you will have very good luck with bets with the bookie. Bets that you didn't even realise you had placed. They will be placed on your behalf after a race has completed. To the tune of, shall we say, $10,000 or so winnings per month.'

Clever, thought Jennifer. She would receive $120,000 per year with no paper trail. If the funds were ever questioned, they would be gambling winnings, with no way to prove otherwise.

'Do I have an alternative?' asked Jenny.

'Only a very painful one.'

'Then I accept.'

'A wise choice. Then I think our discussions are over for this evening. I will have one of my lieutenants contact you. We will not meet again but, just to be quite clear, it would be your worst nightmare if we do ever have to meet again.'

With that Jenny rose from the table and headed towards the door. The Exporter in the corner of the room had never spoken. She had not even detected him move in his seat.

As Jenny returned to the car, the large man outside gave her back her phone. She knew that the watchers on the other side of the bay would be relieved to see her leaving.

She drove in silence around the bay to Coromandel town. She would not turn on the radio comms or use her phone as there was no way to check to see if her car had been bugged while she was in the meeting.

It was now one in the morning and, as she drove through Coromandel township, and took the road to the town of Thames, it was all very quiet. The only vehicle she saw was a large motorhome that pulled out behind her.

The winding road between Coromandel and Thames runs along the side of the massive Firth of Thames estuary. After Jennifer had been travelling for about thirty minutes, the motorhome behind her flashed its lights. This was the signal for Jennifer to check carefully the side of the road. Within about thirty seconds Jennifer saw a layby up ahead. Standing there was a woman, and Jennifer recognised her as one of her more junior colleagues in the SIS. She was about Jennifer's height and build, wearing a wig identical to Jennifer's hair and had on the same clothes as her.

Jennifer pulled into the layby, did not turn off the engine and got out of the car. With only a nod and no words spoken, the woman got into the driver's seat and drove off.

The car would be driven to a parking garage in Auckland. To any observer by the side of the road, the car passing in the dark would contain a woman looking like Jenny Simpson.

The motorhome had pulled into the layby behind Jenny and she now got in.

Tom, Chuck and the technician all seemed very glad to see her.

'How are you?' asked Tom.

'Fine.'

'Well, then, let's get to the debrief, shall we?' said Tom. He nodded to the technician, who turned on the internal recording device in the motorhome. The contents of the recording would be transcribed at a later date for the official record. Chuck would not speak while the device was on. His presence at the operation would never be noted.

Jennifer started: 'Two visible security guards, one outside and one inside. Two people in the meeting, Chain and the Exporter. The Exporter never spoke or indeed moved during the whole meeting. Quite clever, as it would be difficult to charge him with anything other than simply being present at a meeting. The pitch to Jenny was in two parts. To grease the importation of a hundred firearms and future drug shipments. That was just the lead-in. But the real money, and why the Exporter is present, is the onward shipment of firearms. The arms would arrive in New Zealand from, no doubt, a country that would be a red flag for arms importation. Jenny would then facilitate, before any inspection in New Zealand, their onward journey to a third country. The arms, still labelled as machine parts, would then arrive in the third country. All of the documentation would show that they originated from the far safer country of New Zealand, hence making it much easier to arrange their importation and clearance through that country's Customs.

Tom asked the question he knew Chuck was burning to ask but could not while the tape was running. 'Any indication that this has anything to do with APEC99?'

After a moment's thought, Jennifer replied, 'None that I can see.'

'Fine, we will stop the recording there,' said Tom as he glanced at the technician. 'We will conduct a fuller debrief tomorrow as I am sure we could all do with some sleep.'

With the recording device turned off, Chuck leaned forward to Jennifer. 'Are you sure there is no hint of an APEC99 link?'

'As I have stated for the official record,' she said with just a hint of irritation. 'No indication in the dialogue or the scheme that Jenny is to be involved with that this is anything more than importation of a small number of illegal firearms and drugs with the real purpose being the facilitation of onward transfer of firearms shipments.'

Chuck leant back in his seat. 'Good, now where to from here?'

Tom reflected for a moment. 'There appears to be little security intelligence interest in this matter. While there is a criminal conspiracy to corrupt a Customs officer, for police to lay charges, this would require Jenny here to give evidence in open court and that is not going to happen. It would also require the SIS to state why the investigation started.'

Chuck moved uncomfortably in his seat.

Tom continued: 'I think it is time for Jenny Simpson and all her records to disappear. When the bookie's contact at the IRD checked Jenny's records, he tripped a tracing application so we now know who he is. Chain is a bright boy. When he can't find Jenny, he will ask the bookie to have her IRD tax records checked again to see if she is still employed. When the answer comes back that there are now no records of her at all, he will recognise that there is only one agency in New Zealand with the power to clandestinely delete IRD records. He will know our interest was because of the Exporter and that little partnership will be over.

'Just one loose end...' said Jennifer.

'Ah, yes, the mole in the IRD. Well, I think we will keep that as a little bonus from the operation,' said Tom.

Jennifer, completing the thought, said, 'I think I will pay Mr Mole a visit. He now works for me unless he wants to go to prison. Could be very useful in the future to know who is into serious debt with the bookie.'

'Quite so,' said Tom.

With that, the technician moved to the driver's seat of the motorhome and they headed off for the slow two-hour drive to Auckland Airport.

Tom and Jennifer would be on the next day's red-eye flight to Wellington. Chuck Smith, 'tourist', would be on the next available flight to the USA.

Chapter Twenty-Five

It was a cold July winter's day as the flight left Auckland for Queenstown. As they were heading south, it was going to get colder. The direct flight would take about two hours and Brad, even more than usual, was not looking forward to it. Joe, Brad and Tom had been joined on this venue assessment trip by their American Secret Service colleagues, Beauford and Peter. Queenstown had been confirmed as the location for the US President to play golf on the first day of his state visit.

As Brad and Joe knew, it was much easier to undertake these venue assessments with the lead security personnel of each country and resolve any concerns that may arise there and then. The alternative was that the host security team and the visiting security team would review separately, probably get two different views on threats and possibilities and spend the next three months in a pissing contest as to who was right.

The relationship with the two affable, but very professional, Americans had gone well. The five of them had found themselves enjoying each other's company. The fact that the country threat level in New Zealand was one of the lowest in the world helped considerably. It certainly meant that the agents could move around without armed guards and the constant threat of murder or kidnap. However, all five understood well that a US presidential visit 'imports' its own threat level.

The compromise brokered by Brad, and now confirmed by legislation, regarding the importation and carrying of firearms by US Secret Service agents had also done a lot to raise his standing with the US delegation.

As the plane levelled out heading south from Auckland, Beauford had raised himself from his seat in the row in front and turned to look at Brad. He had been told of Brad's dislike of flying and had thought to engage him in a little light conversation to take his mind off the aluminium tube hurtling along 30,000 feet above the ground that he currently found himself in.

'I have just worked out why you guys are so confused all of the time,' said Beauford. 'You drive on the wrong side of the road, your seasons are all back to front; whoever heard of Christmas in the middle of summer? And to cap it off you play your version of football without a helmet.'

Brad said nothing but gave Beauford a look that was an unmistakable 'Go away'. After a moment Beauford said with a smile, 'Okay, talk later,' and sat back down in his seat.

Joe had been to Queenstown many times for work and pleasure. He thought it was one of the most stunningly beautiful places in the world, set as it was on the mirror-like Lake Wakatipu, surrounded by mountains; it was a view agreed with by many tourists and travel writers.

In keeping with the feeling of natural awe that Queenstown evokes, the landing there is one of the most difficult in the world for a commercial airport. Depending on your appreciation of flying, it is either an experience to be remembered forever or twenty minutes of abject terror.

This approach to the airport involves the pilot descending into a valley and then following its twists and turns while continuing to descend to the runway. As you near the airport, the view from either side of the aircraft looks straight into the side of what looks like a very close mountain range.

Brad, not surprisingly, had chosen the aisle seat and had spent the descent stoically focused on the back of the seat in front. Both Joe and Tom knew to leave him alone at this stage of a flight.

The party of five departed the plane via stairs into a light snowfall. Like the other passengers, they hurried the short distance to the entrance to the terminal building. With no checked bags, they headed straight to the car rental office to pick up their people-mover vehicle.

After a short drive, they were introducing themselves to the Police Area Commander in the brand-new Queenstown Police station. The new building, which had been opened the previous year, was quite magnificent and was not out of place in relation to the houses of multi-millionaires whose homes and estates dotted the area. It is a police courtesy throughout the world that, if you are on someone else's 'patch', you announce your presence. It is not that the five of them could not have concluded the visit and left without the introductions, but if you wanted some assistance from the local area commander down the road, and he discovered you had not paid the courtesy, then good luck with that.

After the pleasantries, the small team headed to the Millbrook Resort. Driving through some of the most breathtaking scenery in the world, they soon completed the fifteen-minute drive to the five-star resort located near the old gold rush village of Arrowtown.

The resort and its international golf course are set on 200 hectares of the Wakatipu Basin. The area is bordered by the Crown and Remarkables mountain ranges and Lake Wakatipu. The accommodation is all low-rise and spread over a wide area consisting of luxury studio apartments to resort villas, some run by the hotel and some privately owned.

This mix posed a problem for Peter and Beauford. They preferred whole hotels for venues for the president to stay at, giving them complete control to ensure safety. However, often this was not possible as hotels have contracts with the likes of airlines for flight staff. Even the allure of the publicity of having a President of the United States stay for a day or two does not compare financially with fifteen or twenty flight staff on expenses, staying every night.

They checked into the hotel for the one-night stay and dropped their flight bags in their rooms. The studio apartments were the simplest of the rooms available but were still way better than anything any of them were used to staying in. They were then ferried by golf cart back to the main reception to meet the hotel manager. This would be the highest-profile visitor the resort had catered for and the opportunity for marketing had not been lost on the hotel's owners or senior staff.

The five visitors were ushered into the manager's office. They were joined by the resort's head of security and, following introductions and the arrival of coffee, the manager gave them an overview of the resort and presented each with a ring binder containing maps and resort documentation.

After a brief discussion, it was agreed that the hotel would provide a detailed list of all staff and private home owners on the resort. This list would be updated on a regular basis ahead of the president's visit. The vetting of these two lists and anyone booking accommodation during the president's stay would be the responsibility of Tom for the New Zealand SIS and Peter and Beauford for the Americans. Each would use their own resources and databases to complete the vetting.

It was agreed with the manager that any member of staff who failed the vetting would not be rostered on during the president's visit. The matter of any home owner who failed the vetting was a little more difficult. It might be necessary to try to induce them not to be present during the two days and one night that the president visited. Explanations of an overcrowded resort and offers of free dinners to compensate for staying away were discussed.

The party of seven then headed out on two golf carts to survey the resort.

A spur road containing twenty-four houses was of particular interest to the venue review team. Only four of the houses were privately owned. It was possible these could be rented for the two days. This would allow the Secret Service to close the road and 'own the street' on which the homes stood. The area was bounded by two fairways of the golf course, giving ideal open space for the Secret Service to patrol and provide a secure location.

While the US would bring with them and install more communications functionality for the two days than would be found in most small countries, they were concerned that the ageing hotel switchboard might not meet their and the travelling media's requirements. The hotel manager agreed on the spot to have a new telephone switchboard installed.

Later, at dinner, the five discussed their observations of the day. They started to estimate the security and support personnel required. In broad terms, the numbers would be about 1200 US personnel, 300 New Zealand police and 250 local defence force personnel. They would then need to consider the resources required at the airport and for the route from the airport to the resort. Any last-minute sightseeing or souvenir shopping that the president and his entourage may wish to conduct would also need to be catered for.

Brad asked Beauford, 'How are you going to get him in and out? You know the runway at Queenstown is not long enough to take the Air Force One jumbo.'

'Well,' said Beauford, 'it is too far from Auckland to helicopter him in so we will probably need to fly him here in something a little smaller.'

As they all knew, the highly modified Boeing 747s that most people think are called Air Force One are more than presidential airplanes. They are highly sophisticated command and control centres from which a president could direct a nuclear war, if necessary. They also carry the most highly sophisticated missile defence capabilities of any airplane in the world. The idea is that, in the event of a major conflict, the plane can defend itself and, with the aid of mid-air refuelling, stay in the air and allow the commander in chief to direct the defence of the USA for weeks on end, if necessary.

The US military and Secret Service do not like it if the president is remote from a land-based or airborne facility that provides this functionality.

Brad was well aware of this and, after another sip of the locally produced Pinot Noir and with a slightly mischievous look on his face, said to Beauford, 'So you will bring him in on one of your Gulfstream jets then.' It was Peter who responded in his Southern drawl and with an equally mischievous face: 'We have no such aircraft in our inventory.'

Joe now chipped in. 'So those three that were bought in 1985 under the Reagan administration. I wonder what happened to them?'

The Gulfstream, a twin-engined executive jet, can land on much shorter runways. The three planes that had been purchased had been spotted in various locations in the US and overseas, in the vicinity of a travelling president, often with new paint jobs and tail identification marking. While it was the official US position that they did not exist in the presidential fleet, it was one of the worst kept secrets, and one that many plane spotters throughout the world delighted in exposing.

Beauford, looking for a diplomatic way to move the conversation off this topic, raised his glass and said, 'To the great friendship between the United States of America and New Zealand.' They all raised their glasses and Tom chimed in for the home team: 'You can't put a price on liaison.'

Chapter Twenty-Six

It was 8.30 pm and Laura was following Michelle Roberts. She had been observing her for eight days now and had determined she was quite a loner. She mainly moved back and forth between her home and her job in a marketing company in central Sydney. She shared her home, a simple apartment on the outskirts of the city, with her cat.

When she had followed her this Saturday evening in her car, Laura had parked opposite the downtown carpark that Michelle had pulled into. When she saw her walk to the exit of the parking garage, Laura had then tailed her on foot as she crossed a small park and headed into a brightly lit theatre.

Laura had decided this was looking like her opportunity to engage. She had situated herself in a dimly lit area of the park where she had a good view of the brightly lit theatre entrance. The only issues that might require her to abort her plan was if Michelle left the theatre in the company of others or if there were too many people around in the park.

At 10.15 pm she could see the audience starting to leave the theatre and a few moments later spotted Michelle. She was in the company of a couple about her age. They paused just outside the entrance where they engaged in an animated conversation. Laura watched from the safety of the park intently.

'Come on, blow them off,' she said quietly to herself.

As if they had heard her, which of course they hadn't, the three stopped chatting, exchanged hugs and kisses and the couple headed off down the road. Michelle crossed the road to the small park and headed back down the path to the parking garage.

Laura, who was dressed in dark pants and jacket, fell in about twenty metres behind Michelle and kept pace with her. Looking all around, Laura confirmed that there was no one else in sight. She reached into her pocket and pulled out a thin, black balaclava which she placed over her head and face. She then extracted from her pocket, and extended, a telescopic steel baton.

Accelerating to a very quiet run, she came up behind Michelle. At the last moment Michelle heard a noise and started to turn her head. The steel baton came down with force and struck her just behind the left ear. She fell to the ground silently and unconscious.

Laura gave two more precise blows with the baton and then, picking up the handbag that Michelle had dropped, moved quickly off the path to some nearby trees.

When she was far enough away, she looked in the handbag, extracted a set of keys and a wallet and secured them in the zip pockets of her jacket. She left the mobile phone in the handbag and threw it under a nearby bush.

Removing her reversible jacket, she turned it inside out and put it back on. Now in a white jacket, she extracted a white baseball cap from a pocket and put that on as well.

She could hear a commotion starting to rise from the path fifty metres away. The unfortunate Michelle had been discovered. Laura now broke into a steady, but not fast, run in the opposite direction from the path. If anyone had caught a glimpse of the black-clad assailant, all the better. They would not mistake them for the white-jacketed and capped woman out for her late-night run in the park.

Laura slowed to a steady walk as she neared her car parked opposite the parking garage. As she did, a police car with lights flashing, siren going and moving at speed raced past her heading into the park.

Laura sat in her car and reviewed the contents of Michelle's wallet. Credit cards, some cash and the only item that Laura was interested in, Michelle's driver's licence. She returned the purse to her pocket. She would dispose of the purse and all of its contents, other than the driver's licence, somewhere it wouldn't be found later.

She then drove steadily to Michelle's apartment,

parking on the opposite side of the road. Laura made her way casually to the main entrance. Looking all around, she satisfied herself that no one was about to enter or leave the block. She entered the main door using Michelle's keys, took the lift to the eighth floor and, again checking that the corridor was empty, she let herself into the apartment.

All was quiet inside. She locked the door behind her. It would not do to be surprised by anyone. She gave the very friendly cat that greeted her a gentle rub on the head.

She quietly looked around as she put on a pair of latex gloves. There would be no trace that she had been there and no fingerprints left behind. The desk by the far side of the lounge seemed the obvious place to start. In the second drawer, she found what she was looking for. Michelle's passport.

Pocketing the passport, Laura left the apartment as she had found it, locking the door behind her. When the police came to check, as they would, there would be no indication that anyone had been there. She hoped they remembered to look after the cat.

At about the same time in Sydney's Central Hospital a detective constable who had just come on shift was talking with the admitting nurse in the Accident and Emergency department.

'Just following up on the incident in the park. Did she have any ID on her?' he asked.

'You mean the mugging?' said the no-nonsense nurse.

'Could well be,' came the response.

'No ID,' said the nurse. 'She has managed to tell us her name is Michelle Roberts but not much else.'

The detective noted this in his book. 'Can I speak with her?'

'Not right now. They are just about to take her to X-ray. But if the X-rays confirm the initial diagnosis, then you will have plenty of time to talk with her.

'What do you mean?'

'Two fractured legs just below the kneecap. She won't be going anywhere for quite a few weeks.'

'Ouch,' said the detective.

Chapter Twenty-Seven

The Taiwanese immigration officer liked this assignment. As the officer stationed at the VIP lounge of Taipei Airport, he got to meet the rich and famous as they made their way to their private jets. Much better than dealing with thousands of members of the public in the main immigration hall. He studied the passport he had been given and then looked at the face of the woman in front of him. The face looked the same as the passport photograph, eyes the same colour, which were not as important for identification as they could soon be changed with 'coloured' contact lenses. However, the hair was the same colour and style, and the glasses were the same. With that he stamped the passport, returned it to the woman and in good English said, 'Have a good trip Ms Roberts.'

Laura made her way to the group of four men standing

by the window of this small but beautifully appointed departure lounge.

The 'Pig' greeted her with that leering smile she had come to expect.

'Gentlemen, may I introduce...'

He paused. At this point, Laura thought he was going to introduce her by her real name but, as the look on his face moved from a leer to a sneer, she realised he was toying with her. She returned his look with a glare of her own.

'Michelle,' he finally said.

Each of the other three men nodded and smiled at Laura.

Laura gestured to the Pig to move to one side and said, 'Sir, one private matter to discuss with you before we take off for Auckland.'

'Of course, excuse me for a moment, gentlemen,' and the two of them moved to a quiet corner of the lounge.

Laura fixed him with a gaze and said, 'Let me be very clear. As per our agreement, you will fly me into and out of New Zealand with your little business delegation here. In the event that anything should inhibit my safe travel, a document detailing the events, including photographs, of the ... mishap in the Vancouver Hotel room two years ago will be sent to both the Canadian and Taiwanese Police.'

All expression drained from the Pig's face.

Laura was confident that there would be no more toying with her, and she went on.

'I should also remind you that should you be

questioned after the APEC event about me, you will tell
them you hired Michelle Roberts and give them a copy of
the Michelle Roberts' CV I have given you. That is all you
will tell them. Should they find me through information
given by you, we will both be in a lot of trouble. Do I make
myself clear?'

'Yes.'

At this point an exquisitely dressed hostess
approached them and said in Chinese, followed by
flawless English, that their plane was ready. No vulgar
public address systems in this lounge.

The flight was uneventful. Laura took a single seat and left
the men to their noisy conversation in Chinese. She
continued to wear the coloured contact lenses and clear
lens glasses throughout the flight. Best that she stay in
character for the businessmen.

It was just on 4 pm when they arrived at Auckland
Airport on 6 September 1999. The heads of state would
not start showing up for another four days. There were,
however, several hundred officials of the twenty-one
countries and several thousand members of the world's
media already in town to get the party started.

They proceeded to the Auckland Airport VIP lounge
for immigration and Customs clearance.

The clearance procedures were friendly but very
efficient. Considerable time was taken in processing the

passports. When it was Laura's turn, the immigration officer asked for her address and she gave Michelle's in Sydney. The added advantage in Laura travelling on an Australian passport was that no visa was required, as Australia and New Zealand allow reciprocal unhindered travel and residency for their citizens.

Obviously interested in an Australian woman travelling with four Taiwanese men on a private jet from Taipei, he casually enquired, 'And what about those Roosters?'

'Don't care,' said Laura. 'I am a Rabbitohs girl myself.'

Satisfied that she knew her Sydney rugby league teams and with no reason to doubt the passport she had presented, he stamped it and gave it back to her with a cheery 'Welcome to New Zealand'.

Laura collected her suitcase and, after clearing Customs and biosecurity, she gave a polite wave to the four men she had travelled with and headed to the ladies toilet to change out of the business suit into something more casual. She removed the glasses and coloured contact lenses and carefully packed them away. She did not expect to need them again until her departure. She put on a pair of jeans, T-shirt and trainers. The addition of a blonde wig and sunglasses completed the transformation to Christine Stephenson.

As she left the terminal building to catch the shuttle bus to the motorhome rental company, she passed the Pig and his three colleagues getting into a hire limousine. None of them recognised her, which made Laura smile to herself. Within a few minutes she was on a bus taking her to the motorhome rental company just outside the airport.

'Hello,' said the fresh-faced young man behind the counter as she entered the office.

'Indeed, it is,' said Laura. 'I have a two-weeks booking. My name is Christine Stephenson.'

'Passport, driver's licence and credit card please,' said the youth, wearing a badge introducing him as Bruce.

'My passport and driver's licence,' said Laura, 'but there is a problem with my credit card. It was stolen. I spoke with your manager a couple of days ago and he said it would be okay to pay the rental and bond in cash.'

'Oh yes, I see that noted on your booking,' said Bruce as he looked at his computer screen. 'No problem.'

He gave a casual look at the passport and returned it to her. He then looked at the driver's licence.

'That's all fine. Including the bond payment, that will be 1450 New Zealand dollars, please.'

Laura placed the large sum on the counter.

As Bruce processed her rental booking, she thought through, as she had a hundred times before, how the search for her would proceed when she had completed her task.

Police would find the motorhome, or what was left of it, soon after the incident. They would, in time, trace it to the rental company. They would interview the young man in front of her now and he would supply a vague description of a blonde woman in her thirties. There would be no record of Christine Stephenson having arrived at Auckland Airport, or any other port in New Zealand.

The next step for police would be to review the records of all women who had arrived at Auckland Airport that day in the age range thirties to forties. One of those women would be Michelle Roberts. After requests to the Australian Federal Police, Michelle Roberts would eventually be found in a hospital bed in Sydney.

Satisfied they now knew the alias of the person who had entered New Zealand that they were looking for, the search would focus on the Michelle Roberts who had left on a private jet as part of a business group to Taiwan.

An interview with the Pig would reveal a fake CV and explanation that she was a beautiful assistant, who had not undertaken much secretarial work, but had provided more athletic companionship. The Pig knew to stick to this story or spend the rest of his life in jail for the murder in Vancouver.

Further enquiries would reveal that Michelle Roberts left Taiwan the same day as she arrived in the country on a flight to Laos.

Despite the enormous round-the-clock efforts of New Zealand Police and the undoubted full cooperation of the might of the US Secret Service and all of the US Intelligence agencies, Laura estimated that the fastest their investigation could take would be forty-eight hours. She needed twenty-four hours from leaving New Zealand to disappear in Laos. After a period of backpacking, Laura

Cosgrove would cross the land border to Vietnam and make her way back to Sydney.

She was woken from her thoughts by the voice of the young man.

'That all looks great. If you come with me, I will show you around the motorhome.'

'You really don't need to trouble. I had a van like this a few months ago and I am very familiar with it,' lied Laura, eager to spend as little time conversing with Bruce as possible.

Pleased to be relieved of going through the motorhome orientation script for the hundredth time that week, he said, 'Great, well you have a wonderful holiday.'

'Thanks,' said Laura, as she took the keys and headed to the neat row of vehicles.

Within a few minutes Laura had located her motorhome from the number plate on the key fob, loaded her bags and was heading north away from the airport.

Chapter Twenty-Eight

The Hercules transport aircraft of the Royal Australian Air Force made its final turn towards Whenuapai Airport on the outskirts of Auckland. Captain Alex Conrad had flown into the Royal New Zealand Air Force base many times. The New Zealand SAS and Australian SAS trained together and had fought together in various conflicts. They were currently serving together in Afghanistan.

His plane was loaded with sixteen members of the Australian SAS and the large amount of equipment and firearms they travelled with for such an engagement. They would be met at the airport by the commanding officer of the New Zealand SAS and his senior police liaison officer. The clandestine nature of the work undertaken by the SAS meant that there would be no paperwork to complete. A salute followed by a handshake between the detachment commander for the Australians and the commander of the New Zealand troop would be all that was required. An unmarked police car would then escort the Australian contingent and their equipment to the SAS base in Hobsonville, a short drive away. No requirement for highly public acts of Parliament for these foreign nationals to bring their firearms onto New Zealand soil.

As he levelled out for the final approach, Alex thought about the last couple of months. Just about anything could be bought in Afghanistan for the right price. Either from the Taliban or the Afghan security forces, it did not matter. Alex had been flying in and out of Afghanistan for ten years. The Australian SAS had been on the ground even before the Russians had finally departed in 1989. This fact was not, of course, known to the Australian public or most Australian parliamentary members.

The story given to the Afghan middleman of the Australian SAS wanting to acquire a Stinger missile had been plausible enough. However, Alex suspected he did not really care. The sight of US$300,000 in the suitcase, $50,000 of which was his cut, had been all he had needed to work his contacts and arrange a meeting with the seller. Alex had, of course, kept $200,000 in reserve for those 'incidental expenses'.

Within two days of his initial contact with the businessman, a meeting was scheduled to exchange 'merchandise'. There might be a war on, but business was business. A liaison with a pick-up truck had taken place about fifty miles outside of Kabul. As agreed, there had been four men in each party. Alex had the businessman with him and two heavily armed Afghan special forces soldiers, moonlighting for a little extra cash on the side. They would ask no questions. The other group at the meeting consisted of four Taliban soldiers who had arrived in a pick-up truck.

The meeting had been business-like. On the back of the pick-up truck under a tarpaulin were two cases about two metres long. One contained the Stinger missile and the launcher unit was packed in the other. As Laura was very well aware, Alex was an expert on the Stinger missile. As the main threat to his flights in and out of Afghanistan, he had undertaken a number of training courses on how they operated and their performance.

With a gesture of his hand, the lead seller had invited Alex to check the merchandise. Alex loaded the missile into the launcher and set the control to ready to fire. The missile ran its self-test routine and the light indicated it was ready to fire. This meant that the specialist battery was operating and the guidance electronics within the rocket were operative.

As the Taliban did not have an air force to protect, they did not care who had Stingers.

Removing the missile from the launcher unit, Alex returned both to their cases, signalling his satisfaction to the businessman.

The businessman retrieved the briefcase of cash from the car. The tallest of the Taliban, who appeared to be the leader, checked the contents of the case and, with a nod, the deal was complete. Alex and the contact carried the two cases from the truck and placed them in their Land Cruiser, being careful not to cross the line of fire of their two watchful bodyguards. With everyone back aboard, the two vehicles headed back in the direction from which they came.

As the captain of a flight carrying clandestine special forces, it was Alex's responsibility to sign off on the manifest for each flight. He knew that no one would question the two unmarked old cases on the flight back to Australia. Likewise, he was not questioned about the same two cases that were now stored just separate from the many other unmarked old cases accompanying the SAS solders on their way to New Zealand.

They landed at Whenuapai, the salute and the handshake between the two officers took place and six unmarked white panel vans pulled up at the tailgate of the Hercules. Alex placed himself, as he always did, in the main cabin by the door to the cockpit. From here he, as usual, could observe the unloading of the plane. The SAS troopers always unloaded their own equipment. The boxes of equipment, firearms and cases of ammunition were loaded into the vans. As one of the troopers moved to pass Alex and towards the two cases strapped to the side of the cabin, Alex casually said, 'Not those two, mate; they are with me.'

A nod from the junior trooper and he turned, walked down through the now empty cabin, down the ramp Land got into one of the vans with his colleagues. With the two officers in the back of the unmarked police car, the convoy of six vans plus car pulled slowly away. No flashing lights or sirens for the short drive to the SAS base at Hobsonville.

Alex had requested his own vehicle. The SUV pulled up by the plane driven by a very young member of the New Zealand Air Force. The driver got out and approached Alex, who was now at the foot of the tailgate of the Hercules. After a sharp salute, the young aircraftman asked, 'Are you Captain Conrad, sir?'

Alex retuned the salute. 'Indeed.'

Without any more formalities, the aircraftman handed Alex the keys to the SUV, turned on his heels and walked smartly back towards the main building.

Alex informed his co-pilot to complete the shutdown routine with the crew as he was required elsewhere. This was not the sort of flight crew that asked too many questions, especially of a senior officer. Alex loaded his bags and the two cases into the SUV and headed off towards the main gate to depart the airport.

He was stopped by the security personnel at the gate. On inspecting his credentials, and having just let through a car and six white vans with instructions not to search any of them, they waved him through.

Alex turned out of the airport and headed north. He picked up State Highway 1 and drove for thirty minutes. He exited the highway and followed the sign to Mahurangi Regional Park, one of the smaller and less well-known regional parks. As Alex pulled into the camp site, he noticed a slender woman with short hair. Wearing shorts and T-shirt, she was sitting in a camp chair next to a motorhome reading a book.

He pulled the SUV up next to the motorhome. The woman looked up from her book and, as she rose from the chair, smiled and waved at Alex. Alex got out of the SUV and, as he said, 'Lovely to see you,' she gave him a friendly hug and a kiss on the cheek. To anyone watching, just two friends catching up.

'Do you have the supplies?' Laura asked in her straightforward manner.

'Indeed, I do. And, before you ask your second question, I encountered no problems whatsoever.'

'Then let me help you into the motorhome with them,' Laura said with a smile.

Alex opened the tailgate of the SUV and they each took out one of the long cases. Alex also picked up a small rucksack and after entering the motorhome Laura locked the door behind them.

The curtains were all drawn, but it was a bright day and no need for any of the lights to be on. They placed the two cases on the table and each of them opened a case.

'Nice move with a motorhome,' commented Alex. 'Go where you want, stay where you want and no nosy hotel receptionists or credit card trails for anyone to follow. Much safer for transporting two large cases anywhere with ease.'

Laura did not respond but started to inspect the contents of each case. She extracted both pieces of equipment and, skilfully, loaded the missile into the launcher and powered up the launcher's system. If this had been almost anyone else, Alex would have asked if they knew what they were doing. But he knew that Laura would have made herself fully familiar with the operation of the missile.

After a few moments the launcher light indicated that the Stinger had completed its self-checks and was ready to fire. Laura powered down the launch unit, extracted the missile from the launcher unit and replaced both back in their cases.

'And the other items?' asked Laura.

'Absolutely,' said Alex. He opened his rucksack and extracted a small box about half the size of a shoebox. He opened it and took out the device inside.

'This contains about a half-kilo of plastic explosive, a small container of white phosphorus and a detonator. The detonator has a mercury tilt-switch and a delay timer that can be set for up to ninety-nine hours. You set the device like this.' Alex proceeded to show Laura how to set the timer and arm the device.

'When you extract this pin, the timer will commence its countdown. The mercury tilt-switch will not activate for ten minutes. The delay is to ensure that you are nowhere near when the switch activates. After the ten minutes any movement of the device, or the item it is attached to, and it will detonate. If no movement is detected, it will explode when the timer reaches zero. Any questions?'

'Only about the other item,' continued Laura.

Alex smiled and extracted a pistol from the backpack and handed it to Laura.

'An HP,' said Laura, referring to a Browning Hi-power semi-automatic pistol. She inspected the action of the pistol, looked at Alex and said, 'And the clips?'

'Six clips of ammunition,' said Alex but made no move to retrieve them from his backpack.

Laura looked at him and smiled. 'Alex.' He smiled back. They both knew what was going on. There was no way in an exchange like this in a closed and curtained motorhome that he was going to hand her a loaded gun. Friendship and trust only went so far in this business.

'Well, to money, then,' said Laura. 'Shall we?'

She unlocked the motorhome and they exited into the bright sunlight. Laura again locked the door. They headed to the far side of the small campground and the old-fashioned telephone box located there. It would have been simpler to use a mobile phone. But that would leave a direct link between the number they were about to call and a mobile phone account. Even acquiring prepaid mobile phones was becoming more difficult nowadays, requiring ID to be produced.

Laura entered the telephone box and with her handful of New Zealand coins, dialled the number of her private banking contact at the bank in the Cayman Islands.

After two rings, a polite voice at the other end of the phone said, 'Good day, account number please.'

Laura gave the eleven-digit number.

'Pass phrase please.'

Laura recited one of the lines from her favourite poem: 'Into the valley of death rode the one hundred and fourteen.' The variation from the number 600 in Tennyson's original poem regarding the Charge of the Light Brigade, a little added security

'Thank you, madam, and how may I assist you today?'

'I would like to enact the instant transfer of funds previously detailed,' said Laura.

'Of course, madam, may I just confirm this transfer is for one million US dollars into account number 239-7856123-9 at the Switzerland Cantonal Bank.'

'That is correct.'

'I am enacting that transfer now.' He paused for a few seconds. 'I confirm that the transfer is complete.'

This was international private banking at its best, or worst, depending on which side of law enforcement you were working on.

Laura hung up and exited the phone box and, as Alex passed her to make his call, she gave him the remaining coins.

After a few moments, Alex came out and, with a smile, said to Laura, 'All confirmed. An absolute pleasure doing business with you.'

They moved back towards Alex's car. He opened the driver's door and took a brown paper sandwich bag from under the driver's seat. The bag contained six magazines of ammunition for the pistol. 'The last of your provisions as ordered,' he said.

Laura took the bag.

As Alex checked to make sure no one was about, he said, 'You do know that the Stinger has limitations. The three-kilo high-explosive warhead packs a punch that will take out any single-engine jet, which is fine against fighter jets or helicopters, but against a multi-engine passenger plane it may not bring it down.'

He went on, 'If, for example, it was a Boeing 747, like the one used by the US President, and your missile is not brought down by the extensive counter measures, then the engines being spaced so far apart mean that you will likely just take out a single engine. Those babies can fly perfectly well on three or even two engines.'

Laura looked at Alex. 'Pleasure doing business with you also, Alex.'

'Fine.'

Alex got into his car and as he started to drive away, he saw in the rear-view mirror a broadly smiling Laura by the motorhome giving him a cheery wave goodbye.

After entering the motorhome and closing the door, Laura placed the two cases and explosive device in storage bays underneath the main seating area. She loaded the pistol with one of the magazines, pulled the slide to put a bullet in the chamber ready to fire and, after ensuring the safety catch was on, placed the pistol in the glove compartment.

She then opened the curtains and moved outside. To anyone passing, the bath towel appeared to have been placed casually to dry on the back of the motorhome. Likewise, the chair at the front on which she had been sitting while reading her book. In truth, they had been strategically placed to obscure the front and back number plates. There had been no point in giving Alex more information than he needed. She returned to her seat outside in the sun and the book, no longer merely a prop to discourage anyone from engaging her in conversation. After the successful arrival of her deliveries, she might now actually enjoy reading it. She might even take a relaxing swim in the inviting gulf waters later. Everything was going well, and she had time on her side.

Chapter Twenty-Nine

Aircraft had been arriving at Auckland Airport for days carrying trade ministers, foreign ministers, secretaries of state and latterly heads of state and their spouses. This amounted to eighty visiting VIPs representing twenty countries.

There were so many aircraft that Auckland International Airport had had to lay several football-pitch-sized areas of concrete parking to try to accommodate them. Even then there was not enough space and many planes had discharged their passengers and then flown off to other airports around New Zealand to be parked. Not the usual airport parking problem that most visitors to an airport consider.

Brad, Joe and Superintendent Bolt were located in the police operations room at the airport. The main police command and control point was based in the city. From their current vantage point four floors above the tarmac, they could clearly see the large blue and white Boeing 747, seemingly hung in the clear sky in the distance. They had been joined in the control room by US Secret Service Special agent Peter Timmons. It had been important not to advertise the presence of the US Secret Service agent in the police airport control room. Security delegation members of each country, or economy as the Chinese still insisted on calling them, were watching carefully to see what the others were offered. Almost like handing out sweets to children, you had to be very careful to keep everyone the same. Or make sure that no one else observed when one child gets the extra sweet.

The presence of Peter Timmons in the control room was not simply a result of the close working relationship and confidence built up by the police team and Secret Service over the previous eighteen months. It was essential security practice for the arrival of the American president who had the highest threat level of any of the attendees.

Peter was in direct secure radio contact with Beauford who was the Secret Service officer in control on the tarmac. Peter was also one of a dozen US security personnel from a range of agencies who reported directly to Beauford at this stage. If any one of them raised a concern about the arrival, it would be Beauford who would contact the pilot on Air Force One to abort the landing and fly to the alternate airport. There, a second detachment of Secret Service agents were already in position. Needless to say, everyone hoped they would not be needed.

The police team left Peter alone by the window and did not speak with him. His role was to observe them. Any communications to the control room or anything resembling a commotion among the staff and Peter would instantly investigate and inform Beauford. At various points, Peter simply raised the cuff of his jacket to his mouth and spoke a single word into the concealed microphone. This series of codewords simply told Beauford that Peter was not compromised or under any form of duress and that all was well from his vantage point.

The big plane seemed to hang gracefully in the air before it caressed the runway to touch down and roll to its exact predetermined stopping point. The ground staff, under very close supervision, rolled out the staircase and the red carpet. After one more check from Beauford, and having received a dozen correct codewords, he gave the instruction that the door to the aircraft could be opened.

The dignitaries in the welcome committee moved out to their allotted places by the red carpet. The two dozen Secret Service agents moved into their exact positions and then, displaying the utmost charisma, a waving and smiling Bill Clinton appeared in the aircraft doorway. He descended the steps, followed at a discreet distance by his daughter Chelsea and his mother-in-law Dorothy Rodham. Not surprisingly, given the still-swirling Monica

Lewinsky scandal, Hillary had decided not to accompany Bill on this trip.

The reception had been the subject of much discussion between the Secret Service and the New Zealand Police. It was not the usual line of dignitaries who would shake his hand that was of concern. It was the man who would advance on the president, speaking loudly and waving a weapon above his head. The cultural nature of the Maori welcoming ceremony had been explained so that all the Secret Service agents knew what to expect. The uniquely New Zealand welcome commenced and was broadcast around the world.

With the welcomes completed, the president made his way to his black limousine, affectionately known as the Beast.

The convoy of thirty-four vehicles assembled and headed to the airport exit. The function of some of them was obvious, such as the police cars with flashing lights at the front and the precautionary ambulance at the tail of the convoy. It is left to the imagination the purpose of some of the blacked-out vans.

The convoy sped down roads and a motorway closed to all other traffic. In precisely thirty-four minutes it arrived at the entrance to the Stamford Plaza Hotel in downtown Auckland. On arrival the presidential car entered the rear entrance leading to the underground parking garage.

As the TV cameras rolled and the photographers' flashes brightened an already sunny day, the world's media positioned at the main entrance to the hotel failed to get the arrival photographs they had waited several hours for. No one noticed the new interior decorative wall just though the large glass facade of the hotel entrance which obscured the view of the cigar shop.

Chapter Thirty

The seven key members of the APEC security team had all moved into the same downtown hotel for the five-day duration of the event. Not that they expected to see much of their hotel rooms. The event moves very fast and each of them knew they would get very little sleep. Twenty-hour days would be the norm.

The APEC leaders' annual event had settled into a set format for most days. A working lunch and conference day, a formal dinner, a photograph of all of the leaders usually wearing the same silly shirt or outfits as dictated by the home nation and a final Joint Communiqué. It is often the bilateral meetings arranged between leaders where more serious matters of state can be discussed. If there are tensions between countries, arranging a face-to-face meeting can prove diplomatically difficult and telephone calls can prove ineffective. However, the APEC leaders' meeting allows countries to arrange bilateral leaders meetings on neutral third-party territory and often at short notice. This is not something that can often be achieved in the normal course of world events.

From the security perspective, moving the eighty-four VIPs around a city can be an enormous challenge. There are, in effect, two types of motorcade movement. The first involves scheduled movements such as getting all of the leaders to the formal dinner. This has to be done in a highly choreographed way so that the host leader and the first arrival are not left standing around for hours before the last of the twenty leaders turns up.

The second style of motorcade movement is the unscheduled event. These often occur due to bilateral meetings between two leaders arranged at the last moment. The threat to these types of motorcades is slightly reduced due to the fact they have not been publicly advertised months in advance.

Then there are the instant variations, such as the Canadian Prime Minister deciding at the last moment that, as it was such a nice day, he would walk the twenty minutes to the lunch venue. All very good for his health, but protocol dictates that the entire motorcade follow him through the city centre. Of course, the motorcade is now travelling at walking pace.

Then there are the political considerations. The right to peacefully protest is held quite sacred in most democracies, but not all members of APEC are democracies. Chinese officials and bodyguards are literally on pain of death to ensure that their president is not exposed to people protesting against him.

The working lunch, a staple of each APEC meeting, was held in a downtown hotel. Brad, Joe and Charles were in the foyer of the hotel awaiting the arrival of the first leader. Prime Minister Shipley was waiting by the red carpet, surrounded by senior New Zealand diplomats and members of her Department of Prime Minister and Cabinet. One of the senior diplomats, who had been on the phone, broke away from the gaggle and hurried towards Charles.

'Trouble coming our way boss,' said Brad.

As the senior diplomat arrived, he blurted out, 'There are demonstrators on the road outside the hotel and they have to be moved.'

Charles said, 'Have they crossed the barriers?'

'No,' said the diplomat, 'but they have banners.'

'Banners?' said Charles. 'Well, we had better go and have a look, gentlemen.'

Charles, Brad and Joe headed outside followed by the diplomat who was again on the phone.

On the opposite side of the road behind the four-foot-high steel barriers was a crowd about five deep. Most were just there to catch a glimpse of world leaders. But two banners had been hung on the barriers.

'There,' said the diplomat pointing at the banners, as if he was indicating the gunman on the grassy knoll.

A group of about thirty young Asian individuals stood behind the banners. They were standing quite still and making no noise. The banners declared that they were members of the Falun Gong.

Depending on your point of view, the Falun Gong is either a peaceful semi-religious way of life or a dangerous cult. The Chinese government takes the latter view and persecutes them ruthlessly.

One of the banners stated: 'Falun Gong arrested and tortured in China'.

The diplomat who had followed them out of the hotel took the phone from his ear and stated to Charles: 'That was my counterpart with the Chinese delegation. They will not allow their president to be exposed to this demonstration about lies and demand that the demonstrators are removed immediately.'

Charles looked at the diplomat. 'Well, gentlemen, we had better order up the sergeant with the canister of teargas.' The reference to the debacle in Vancouver was not lost on the diplomat, but, true to his role, he considered his response carefully.

'Well, operational security and safety matters are obviously your decision to make Superintendent. I can only express to you the diplomatic impasse we find ourselves in.' The implications of the diplomat's words were not lost on Charles or his two trusted lieutenants.

Charles, with a nod to the diplomat, said to Joe and Brad. 'Let's take a closer look, shall we, gentlemen?'

When they were out of earshot, Brad said, 'Bloody civil servants. They have a problem and will take no responsibility for the solution.'

Charles smiled at him and said, 'Yes, it is called diplomacy.'

They crossed the road from the hotel where the function was to be held, a road normally teeming with traffic but today there was not a car in sight. As they approached the group of thirty silent protestors, Charles said to Brad and Joe, 'You two hold back will you while I have a chat.'

He then removed his police cap, fixed an easy smile on his face and, in this least threatening manner, approached the diminutive figure standing behind the barrier with the largest of the banners hung over it.

Brad and Joe were close enough to hear the conversation. 'Hello,' said Charles. The short, slim young woman looked to be in her early twenties. They could all see the fear on her face and the tears welling in her eyes.

'You have come to arrest us,' she exclaimed in a faltering voice.

'Why,' said Charles, 'have you done something wrong?'

The question made the girl pause before she said, 'We are protesting.'

'Well, you are in New Zealand and peacefully protesting is not against the law.'

It was obvious from the only slightly diminished fear on the girl's face that this was not the response she had experienced in the past when protesting.

'My name is Charles. What is yours?'

The girl was surprised at the informality and said, 'Ming.'

'Well, Ming, I do have a problem and I was hoping you would be able to help me with it.'

'What is that, sir ... Charles?' said the girl, struggling again with the informality.

'Well, these barriers are here for crowd control and you are not really allowed to hang banners from them.'

The tears welled again in the girl's eyes and she blurted, 'You are going to tear down our banners?'

'No,' said Charles smiling gently, 'but I would like to help you take them down.'

With that, the superintendent and the diminutive leader of the Falun Gong protesters carefully undid the strings holding the banners to the barrier. The superintendent folded the banners as carefully and respectfully as if they were a national flag and handed them to the young protestor.

'Now, Ming, you and your friends stay safe behind the barriers and continue your protest if you so wish.'

With that Charles turned and rejoined his two smiling lieutenants. 'Beautifully done,' said Joe.

'Personally, I think we should have batoned them till their eyes popped out,' said Brad. Charles smiled.

As they approached the diplomat, he said, 'Well done on removing the large banners, but the protestors are still there and visible.'

'If they remain peaceful and behind the barriers, they have every right to be there under New Zealand law.'

'The Chinese delegation will not be happy. I must insist,' said the diplomat.

'Insist on what?' said Charles, cutting him short. The tone was measured and quiet, even polite. But the diplomat stopped, regarded Charles and, through a forced smile, practised over the years, said, 'Of course, Superintendent.'

The Chinese motorcade which had been proceeding at about one quarter walking pace while the 'issue' was resolved was informed of the situation. They accelerated significantly as they sped past the quietly protesting Falun Gong members.

In general, the motorcade movements had been working well. There were 517 scheduled motorcade movements, and about three times that number of last-minute arrangements involving everything from high-level bilateral arrangements to shopping trips. The Police, Auckland Council and the National Government had, at an early stage, decided on a strategy to scare the city workers off the streets. A publicity campaign over the previous months had loudly explained the two days of road closures and likely gridlock in the CBD. This had had the desired effect with many CBD workers either taking the two days off or, in the case of a number of large organisations, being given two days' leave.

Chapter Thirty-One

A world away from Auckland, a different type of police interaction was taking place.

The windowless room in the police station just outside Kabul was thick with smoke. It was emanating from two of the people in the room who were chain smoking. Another person in the room stood quietly in the corner. The fourth and last person was secured to a sturdy wooden chair bolted to the floor in the centre of the room.

Earlier in the day, the man in the chair had been walking in the bright sunlight down the main street of his town, just another day for him to conduct whatever business he could. An unmarked old van had pulled up beside him. Before he could react, two men had jumped out and bundled him inside. This was not the kind of police arrest that would be recognised in most countries around the world.

The chains holding the Afghan businessman in the

chair he now found himself in meant that he could not move his arms or legs. He had been alone in the room for ten hours before he had been joined by the three men. Since they entered the room about forty minutes previously, they had not addressed him or asked him any questions. The only acknowledgement that he was there had come when each of the two men smoking came to the end of their cigarette and then stubbed it out on his forearms. They would then casually light another cigarette and continue their affable conversation with each other.

He winced as one of them approached him again with another nearly complete cigarette. This time the bearded man hovered the cigarette above his forearm just six inches from his skin. He looked the businessman in the eyes and with a slight, almost inviting smile said, 'Would you like me to ask you a question?'

'Yes, yes,' came the eager reply.

'We know that you conduct business with the Taliban. Tell us something useful and we will let you return to your family.'

As he looked at each man in turn, the businessman's eyes opened wide. He knew the penalty he and his family would pay if the Taliban even suspected he was a police informant. He weighed up the minimum amount of information that he could give them that might allow him to get out of this room alive and to be able to stay alive when he returned home.

After a lifetime of negotiating deals in one of the harshest environments in the world, the businessman knew how to recognise who held the power among the group he was negotiating with. He looked again at the quiet man in the corner. While his looks, long beard and attire said he was Afghan, there was something about the way that he carried himself that said he was not. If he were not Afghan, and he was in this room with the police, he would most probably be American.

He also knew that whatever he told them they would want more. So as painful as it might be he would need to delay telling them some details as long as possible.

His mind turned to a transaction several months before. This had been between a Taliban group based far to the south of the country on the Pakistan border and a foreigner. The deal, conducted just outside Kabul, had gone without incident and his cut of the proceeds had been substantial. There was no local Taliban involvement which might mean that he was less likely to get his throat cut if he divulged this secret.

As the two captors in front of him grew impatient, without turning his head, he glanced at the man leaning in the corner and spoke to no one in particular.

'There is the Stinger missile.'

The man in the corner tensed and moved very slightly. The businessman thought to himself, yes, this will do. This was now a business negotiation, even if his two smoking captors in front of him did not know it. It would be a painful couple of days as he slowly revealed the details of the transaction. The final detail he would tell them was that the foreign purchaser had an Australian accent.

The CIA agent in the corner of the room was pleased. Recovery of the American-made and supplied Stinger missiles remained a high priority for the CIA. He had been under pressure from his section chief to produce more intel.

This had been a 'fishing expedition'. They had no firm evidence regarding the businessman other than that he had Taliban contacts.

But apply the right amount of persuasion or, rather, have the Afghan police apply the right persuasion, and some useful information might be forthcoming. He would now be able to send his section chief a report that should keep him off his back for a few days at least.

Chapter Thirty-Two

At about the same time as the interrogation in Afghanistan, Laura Cosgrove was enjoying the fresh sea breeze on her face. She had driven the motorhome south from Auckland to the capital Wellington, situated at the lower end of the North Island. She had boarded one of the Interislander Cook Strait ferries that link the two main islands of New Zealand. In typically practical New Zealand fashion these are named North Island and South Island.

The motorhome was stowed several decks below, neatly surrounded by a dozen other white motorhomes all headed to the 'Mainland', as South Islanders like to call it.

Laura had left Auckland and headed south the day after she had collected her packages from Alex. Auckland was swarming with police and intelligence personnel from around the world. There was no point in her staying in that environment any longer than necessary and risk being recognised by some past colleague.

The drive from Auckland to Wellington takes about nine hours. While she could have driven the distance in a day, she had chosen to spend a night in a quiet free campground near the massive central North Island lake, Taupo. No point in staying in one of the paid campgrounds with its almost inevitable congenial and talkative reception staff who would want to engage Laura in polite conversation.

She would continue as she had from leaving Auckland. The motorhome was self-contained with shower and toilet. As such she was entitled to free park in many locations. She had been paying for all her supplies and fuel for the motorhome in cash. There would be no use of credit cards on this trip leaving an easy trail to follow the chain of payments.

After about two hours crossing Cook Strait, the ferry entered the Marlborough Sounds. The speed of the ferry slowed for the last hour of the journey so as not to produce a large wake that could damage the coastline of the area of outstanding beauty.

Laura would drive directly to Queenstown at the other end of the South Island. It was still three days until the president would arrive for his round of golf and she had preparations to make.

Her mind turned to her friend, and she found herself smiling. Their relationship had started fifteen years earlier. They had both had careers to progress and protect.

Neither of them now regarded their careers with the almost religious fervour that they once had. Recent events for both of them had led them to the course of action they were now on. If successful, in two days' time they would be rich and bound together for the rest of their lives as fugitives. If they failed then life, if they were still alive, would be much less pleasant.

As the small port of Picton came into sight, she was woken from her thoughts enjoying the dramatic 'Sights of the Sounds' by a voice on the ship's Tannoy system asking that all drivers return to their vehicles.

Chapter Thirty-Three

Tom Shape, like everyone else on the team, was working very long hours. His mornings started by reviewing the hundred or so intelligence reports that were being sent to him each day. The reports came in two main types – Signals Intelligence, known as SIGINT, and Intelligence derived by Human Resources, agents on the ground, known as HUMINT. If the reports were being provided by a foreign government, and the majority of what Tom was looking at were, then they would likely be summaries so as not to reveal the source and not indicate the type of intelligence. Tom had been doing this work for many years and risen to a level in New Zealand's Security Intelligence Service where he had been the natural choice to act as the services point-man for APEC99 and coordinate the liaison with all interested agencies, domestic and foreign.

This was the largest undertaking in the Service's

history. Tom was under no illusion that there would be promotions for a successful event but, should there be a failure in intelligence leading to a major incident, his would be the first head to roll.

As he read through his reports, he came across one from the CIA. It was a short summary and gave no indication if the source were SIGINT or HUMINT. The report stated that a Westerner had bought a Stinger missile in Afghanistan. Further investigations were ongoing.

Tom took another drink of his strong morning coffee. Was the Westerner the end client or was this a purchase to order? Probably the latter. A fair amount of local Afghan/Taliban knowledge would be required to safely navigate a purchase like this. Tom filed the information away in his mind and moved on to the next report. It was now 6.30 am and he had forty more reports to get through before the 7.30 am daily briefing of the team.

The briefing took place in the conference room adjacent to the operation command centre in Auckland. This underground facility was a secure location. Charles Bolt, as the operations commander, chaired the meetings. The usual seven members of the APEC planning team attended and, on occasion, some invited guests. The meetings were brief, the shortest having been ten minutes and very focused. Today saw the inclusion of two guests who had invited themselves, the Commissioner of Police and his Deputy. Charles, as ever, took their attendance in his stride.

'Thank you for all being here,' began Charles. 'We are

now in the last days of the major event. Before I ask Sir Reginald to update us regarding the state visits that will follow APEC, does anyone have any issues to raise?'

To ensure there was no reticence on the part of any of his six team members given the presence of the Police Commissioner, Charles went quickly around the table addressing each of his team by their first name. Each either shook their head or said no.

'In that case, I will ask Sir Reginald to give us an update and then the Commissioner may wish to say a few words. Sir Reginald...'

'Thank you, Superintendent. As you are all very aware, the New Zealand government has extended a state visit invitation to the president of the USA. This invitation has been accepted. As well as the official engagements, leisure time has also been included in both Christchurch and Queenstown. The substantive APEC leaders' meeting will complete following the issuing of the formal statement at the Auckland War Memorial Museum tomorrow. The president will then fly to Queenstown the following day, Tuesday. His first engagement will be a round of golf in Queenstown with the prime minister's husband, Burton Shipley. He will then fly to Christchurch on the Wednesday for a series of official visits.'

Chapter Thirty-Four

It was 12 September, two days before the arrival of the US president for his golf game in Queenstown. Laura had stayed the night in Wanaka, a small town not far from Queenstown. After breakfast in the motorhome, she drove into Queenstown and found a day parking spot. Just another of the hundreds of thousands of tourists who visit each year.

Her first stop was a car-hire company. Again using just cash, she rented a car for three days. The car was to be returned to Dunedin Airport. The one added extra was a bicycle rack on the back of the car.

Her next stop was an outdoor sports shop. Given that this area was the outdoor adventure capital of New Zealand, there was no shortage of shops to choose from.

'Hello, can I help?' said the young, tanned, outdoor-type sales assistant.

Laura smiled. 'Yes, I am looking for a mountain bike.'

'Great. Let me show you what we have to offer.'

About twenty-five minutes later, Laura left the store pushing the new mountain bike, cycle helmet and cleated bicycle shoes. She headed for the parked rental car a short distance away and secured the mountain bike on the rack. Throwing the helmet and shoes on the back seat, she headed for a quiet valley location about twenty kilometres outside of Queenstown.

She had been studying detailed survey maps of the area for some weeks. She drove to a valley a short distance away and, on arrival, pulled into the secluded carpark she had identified. This carpark was used mainly by keen walkers in the summer months. It was still early in the season and, as she had expected, there was no one else there.

She unhooked the mountain bike from the back of the car. After one further look around, she locked the car, put on the cycle helmet, clipped her cleat shoes into the pedals and set off on the steep climb up the hill.

She enjoyed the ride, grateful that her fitness levels were up to it. It was a steep walking path. The large tyres and very low gears of the mountain bike were made for this type of ascent. The tracks on the path showed that she was not the first mountain biker to make this climb.

After a little under an hour, she arrived at the crest of the ridge that separated the two valleys. Behind her was the quiet little valley. In front of her was the wide Gibbston Valley, a popular wine-growing area. At the bottom was State Highway 6, which was the main road through Queenstown.

After admiring the view for a few minutes, Laura headed down into the valley towards the state highway. The path was very steep, and she descended slowly as she wanted to have a good look around.

After about ten minutes, the narrow path levelled into a grassed area. This rugged carpark would cater for only four or five cars at most. Walkers would start from here in the summer months.

Laura got off the bike and, placing it on the ground, proceeded to walk around the small carpark. As the map had indicated, there was plenty of room to park the motorhome. During early spring, it was very unlikely that she would be interrupted by any walkers.

At the other end of this level space, a rough vehicle track headed down to the valley floor, about 2000 feet below, and State Highway 6.

Laura had identified this as her primary preferred location. She had seen two other backup locations in case this one was not suitable for her purpose. Satisfied and happy that this location would be perfect, Laura got back on her bike and headed slowly down the track to the state highway. She would take her time – she wanted to make sure there were no hidden obstacles for when she brought the motorhome back up the track the following afternoon, and she did not want to fall off the mountain bike. This was no time to get an injury.

On the valley floor she arrived at the state highway

and turned left to head back to Queenstown and the parked motorhome. She would move the motorhome to one of the free camping areas available on the outskirts of the town and settle in for a quiet night. She was confident that the hire car she had left in the next valley would not be the cause of any concern, even if someone did spot it.

Chapter Thirty-Five

The final day of the APEC meeting went well. The leaders' lunch held at the impressive War Memorial Museum in Auckland had a been a great success. Tom, Brad, Joe and Jennifer had decided to head to Queenstown and be in place before the arrival of the US president. While all of the commercial flights had been booked, this had not been a problem. An arrangement had been put in place regarding senior APEC personnel with the national carrier. A phone call to the Air New Zealand liaison officer was all it took and the four of them were guaranteed to be on the flight. Their tickets would be waiting for them at the check-in counter. When they arrived there, they all studiously ignored the commotion at the next counter where a member of staff was trying to explain to a tourist family of four that, despite the fact they had a confirmed booking, there was no room for them on the plane.

After the two-hour flight from Auckland, they landed at Queenstown. It was the last flight of the day as the difficulty of landing at the airport meant that it was only allowed to operate during daylight hours.

They collected two hire cars for the short ride to the Millbrook Resort. They were pleased to be stopped and checked at the entrance road to the resort by the mixed security detail of police and US Secret Service. Having been security-swept for several days, the resort was in a high-level lockdown awaiting the arrival of the president the following morning. They all had rooms booked but a long night of checking and rechecking of the arrangements put in place was ahead of them.

The control centre for Millbrook had been set up in a large conference room. A joint team of police, SIS and US Secret Service would man the room around the clock until completion of the golf round the following day and the president had left Queenstown.

Joe and Jennifer were standing by the table containing the endless coffee that was a prerequisite of any 24/7 control room. It was 1.30 am and this was the first occasion that they had had for several days to have a private conversation.

'My room is very nice,' said Joe in a hushed voice. 'What is your room number?'

Jennifer looked at him and smiled. 'Really, we have both probably managed fifteen hours' sleep in the last five days and you want to know my room number?'

Joe's expression turned to decidedly sheepish as

Jennifer's smiled broadened and she said, 'I am in twenty-seven.'

Just at that point the door to the control room opened and Clive entered. The limp in his right leg seemed more pronounced as he moved to join Joe and Jennifer by the coffee.

'I hope that is hot and fresh,' said Clive as he moved to pour himself a cup.

'Hold on one second,' said Joe. 'How did you get here? I thought you were going to keep an eye on your soldier boys and girls manning the fences at the museum this afternoon. We were on the last flight into Queenstown Airport. You were not on it and the airport closed about five hours ago.'

'I hitched,' said Clive as he took a sip of coffee.

'And who exactly did you hitch with?' stated Jennifer.

Clive took another sip as he let the suspense build with the two colleagues that he had worked with for the past two years.

'I hitched on one of the two helicopters of the counterterrorism SAS teams who were relocating from Auckland down here to cover the state visit. Very nice of them. It did help, of course, that until a few years ago I used to be their commander.'

'Yes, I can see how that might swing it,' said Joe.

Clive, a little more seriously, continued: 'I probably still would be if it had not been for a training accident. I fell from a rope rappelling from a helicopter. Broke my right hip among other things. So no more SAS for me. The hip really does not like this cold weather either.'

The conversation stopped. It was Jennifer who broke the uncomfortable silence. 'So, what is in store for Captain Clive when we have finished with all this?'

'Somewhere warmer,' said Clive, returning to his more affable self.

Jennifer looked at Clive. He was being reduced from a top-action role to simply wanting to be somewhere warmer. It did not seem right. But then they were all suffering from loss of sleep at the moment. A beach somewhere hot and sunny with Joe for a few days seemed very appealing to her right now.

'Well, that is enough for me for today,' said Jennifer. 'Good night, gentlemen,' and with that she headed for the door.

Joe watched her leave as he calculated how long he would need to remain with the team before he left.

He turned back to look at Clive who was staring at Joe and just smiling. Just then the two of them were joined by Tom and Brad.

After a suitable length of time, Joe bade his colleagues goodnight and headed off into the cold weather of a September night in Queenstown.

In a complex swarming with highly skilled and watchful security personnel, some with night-vision binoculars, Joe now realised he had no idea in which direction room twenty-seven was.

Chapter Thirty-Six

On that same day, Monday, 13 September, Laura had woken after spending a quiet night in a free parking area just outside Queenstown. At midday she had taken the motorhome up the mountain track to the small parking area just below the ridge line. She had driven slowly and very carefully to avoid any accidents. There was no one else in sight.

She spent the afternoon timing the approach of both the commercial aircraft and the three private jets that had flown into the airport. All three had been Learjets, a common sight in New Zealand's fourth busiest airport as the rich and famous visit their ski lodges.

She had practised on the incoming flights of two of the jets, taking the fully assembled Stinger unit from the motorhome and to watch the jets' approach. As they followed the contours of the valley below the motorhome's position, the heat from their engines was visible.

She had lifted the unit to her right shoulder. She found the plane through the simple optics of the launcher unit. At this point she had activated the infrared homing functionality and lined the missile up until the audible tone steadied and confirmed that it had located the target aircraft – or, to be more precise, the infrared heat output from the aircraft's jet engine.

The jet she would be targeting the following day would be a Gulfstream G3 with the call sign Air Force One. Laura had worked through the process she planned to undertake to shoot it down. It was one last confirmation that her planning and logic were correct.

This was no typical Gulfstream G3, however. It might well have countermeasures installed to deal with a land-fired heat-seeking missile. Not as sophisticated as its big brother the 747 jumbo jet, but all of the research that Laura had conducted suggested that these countermeasures would be configured to deal with a missile fired from the ground up towards the plane. Not a missile fired down onto the plane.

In most countries in the world, the Gulfstream travelling with the president on board would be escorted by US Air Force fighter jets. However, as Laura's informant told her, it was considered that this was not necessary in New Zealand: the country's closest neighbour, Australia, is over 1000 miles away. An airborne assault was, therefore, less than unlikely. Also, the handful of very old Skyhawk fighter jets, likely to be retired soon, operated by the New Zealand Air Force were seen as an even more unlikely threat.

At this position on its approach to Queenstown Airport, the Gulfstream would be flying at a landing-approach speed of about 200 mph and at about a height of 1500 feet above the valley floor. This was well within the speed and range limits of the Stinger missile. There were steep mountains to both sides of the valley and the aircraft would be very vulnerable.

The G3 had two engines and Laura would lock the Stinger onto one of them. The effect of the three-kilogram high-explosive fragmentation warhead of the missile exploding in one of the engines would undoubtedly take out the second engine, which was a matter of a few feet away.

At its landing approach speed of 200 mph, the effect of losing both engines would mean that the pilot had no time to react before the plane fell below its 147 mph stall speed, the speed at which this type of aircraft would simply fall from the sky.

The plane would go down very quickly, either crashing into the valley floor or hitting one of the very close valley walls. The engines would be on fire and the chance of anyone surviving such a crash would be zero.

Trying to spot the plane the following day would not be difficult. All other traffic would be stopped from arriving at or departing from Queenstown Airport. Then Air Force One's arrival would be preceded by a transport plane carrying the essential staff that travel with the president. Then, in glorious isolation, the Gulfstream would appear.

Having thoroughly gone through her attack process, Laura then went over her escape route one more time in her mind. The valley with the downed plane would very quickly fill with all types of military, law enforcement and US Secret Service. The helicopters that she knew would be stationed at Queenstown Airport would be scrambled and be over the wreckage in a matter of a few minutes.

Once Laura had fired the missile there would be nothing else that she could do to influence the outcome. Regardless of whether the plane crashed or, for some inexplicable reason she had not thought of, she would need to leave immediately. The mountain bike trip would not take long. She estimated five minutes hard push to the top of the ridge and then fifteen minutes fast downhill to the parked rental car. The drive to Dunedin Airport would take about three hours. She would then return the hire car and board the Pig's waiting private jet for the return flight to Taiwan.

The one last task to complete before she set off on the bike would be to arm the mercury tilt-switch explosive charge. For added impact, she had attached it to the propane gas cylinder located in its own secure compartment accessed from the outside of the motorhome.

She had considered setting the motorhome alight as she departed, but this would bring unwanted attention to her location too soon. She had also considered covering the bright white motorhome in a camouflage net but, if she were spotted prior to the missile launch, it would be a lot more difficult to explain its presence. She did not want to invite questions from any nosy walkers. In the end, she had decided to hide the motorhome in plain sight.

Laura had unscrewed the two number plates and buried them a short distance from the van. Anyone investigating the motorhome would need to open the engine compartment to get the vehicle identification number in order to identify it. This movement of the motorhome would cause the small amount of mercury in the detonator to move. This in turn would cause the mercury to close the circuit between two metal contacts and detonate the device. Between the explosive charge, the now exposed phosphorus burning at 2760 degrees Centigrade and the contents of the motorhome's propane gas cylinder, it would be a devastating explosion and fire.

She estimated that the motorhome would be spotted, likely by a circling helicopter, within thirty minutes of the missile strike. Special forces would then rope down from a hovering helicopter within another fifteen minutes to investigate.

There was a dual purpose to the explosive booby trap attached to the motorhome. The explosion and ensuing fire would remove any forensic evidence in the motorhome. Despite having cleaned it thoroughly, there is no way you could live in a motorhome for a week and remove all the forensic trace evidence.

More importantly, it would create confusion and delay and seriously slow down the investigation, giving Laura the time needed to get out of the country. A medical evacuation team on the specialised helicopter would need to be despatched to extract the dead and wounded from the first arrival team. A third team would then have to be despatched to undertake a far more cautious investigation of the site.

By the time that the authorities had identified the motorhome registration via the number on the smouldering engine block, many hours would have passed.

It would then only be a short time before further investigation with the rental company would reveal it had been rented by a Christine Stephenson. This would be a dead end as no such person existed. In the days that followed, the investigation might well lead police to take a closer look at all persons departing New Zealand following the assassination of the US president. This would lead them to eventually find the unfortunate Michelle Roberts in the Sydney hospital.

By that time Laura planned to be long gone.

Chapter Thirty-Seven

Tom was rudely woken by the oversized hotel alarm clock. It was flashing to tell him that it was 4 am on 14 September 1999. After showering and getting dressed, he made himself a pot of coffee and settled down to read the day's intel reports.

After about twenty minutes he came across an update provided by the CIA. The report from Afghanistan was again short. The code indicated this was the second report on the matter. Further investigation indicated that the purchaser of the Stinger missile had been called 'The Aussie'. Again, no further information on where the Stinger might be now or who the end client might be.

As he read the report, there was a knock on the door. He opened the door to find Captain Clive Robertson standing there.

'Come in my friend,' said Tom with a theatrical low

wave of his hand, 'and what does the green machine have to say this morning?'

Clive smiled at the use of the, not completely flattering, name for Her Majesty's New Zealand Army.

'And a good morning to you, master of the black arts,' he said, taking a seat on the sofa.

Speaking in a more business-like tone, Clive asked, 'Anything new in the despatches?'

'We are expecting Bill to be wheels down in Queenstown at about 10 am.'

'What about you? Anything of interest – that you can tell me about, of course?'

'Nothing standing out,' said Tom before a pause. Then, 'Second report on a Stinger missile that has changed hands in Afghanistan. The purchaser is reported as being called the "Aussie". You don't think that "Carlos the Dingo" out of Wallaroo is masterminding an international terrorist plot, do you?' he asked whimsically. 'Come to think of it, any idea what damage a Stinger missile would do to a Gulfstream G3?' he added, not quite so whimsically.

'Probably quite a bit,' said Clive. 'Is there any suspicion that it has made its way into New Zealand?'

'None, and, if there were the slightest suspicion, the Secret Service would whip Bill onto his big plane and have him out of here before you could say Monica. But I should probably raise this with Beauford. ... But, if you were going to sneak a Stinger missile into New Zealand how would you do it?'

The discussion's tone had turned serious.

'Is that coffee still fresh?' asked Clive, pointing to the jug in the corner of the room.

'Yes, help yourself and you can top mine up while you are there,' said Tom.

'Well,' said Clive, returning to the question, 'it depends on the level of assistance you have access to, I suppose. If you have the help of an embassy, then the diplomatic bag is a possibility.'

They both took a sip of their coffee. Clive went on: 'Hiding it in a shipping container is a bit risky. Quite frankly, it would be difficult to break down so that it did not look like a Stinger missile. It would also be a bit too big for a commercial flight.'

Tom was starting to sweat a little. He asked, 'How many Stingers does the NZDF have?'

'None that we admit to, but the SAS boys do like them,' said Clive.

'So, they get moved around on SAS deployments without anyone knowing too much,' said Tom, raising his left arm and making a couple of circles with it to try to relieve the pins and needles sensation. Perhaps he should have followed all that advice to exercise more after all if he was to undertake these long and stressful missions. Joe had told him that there was a very good gym in the main building, but he had informed him, not too politely, that he was allergic to gyms and preferred to check out the bar.

'Yes, the Special Ops soldiers like them because they

are relatively light in weight and provide excellent defence against helicopters that might be hunting them.'

Tom did not hear the end of the sentence. The cramping sensation in his left arm had now become severe and was spreading across his chest. He was sweating very profusely and starting to feel quite unwell.

The pain in his chest became extreme and he called out to Clive through gritted teeth. 'I need some help. I think I am having...'

At that point, Tom grabbed for the phone, knocked the handset from the base unit onto the desk and fell to the floor.

As he lay on the floor, the pain in his chest now felt like an elephant was sitting on it. He could not talk. He watched as Clive rose slowly from the couch, moved to the desk and returned the telephone handset to the cradle. He then returned slowly and sat on the couch, looking directly at Tom.

As the pain in his chest rose and, just before his eyes closed for the last time, Tom looked straight back at Clive and ... he knew.

Clive rose from the sofa and checked Tom's wrist for a pulse. Finding none, he then took the small empty plastic bottle from his pocket. He went to the bathroom and, using his penknife, proceeded to cut the small bottle into very tiny pieces. When he was satisfied the pieces were small enough, he placed them in the toilet and flushed them away. Satisfied that none of the pieces remained, he flushed the toilet twice more.

He then took a half bottle of digoxin tablets from his pocket, carefully wiped the bottle to remove his fingerprints and then, stooping down over Tom's body, rolled the bottle over two of Tom's fingertips. Having applied Tom's fingerprints to the bottle, and carrying it now in his handkerchief, he returned to the bathroom and placed the bottle in Tom's toilet bag.

There would be no trace of the small plastic bottle containing a highly concentrated cocktail of drugs based around digoxin, prescribed widely for various heart conditions. The effect of Clive's cocktail of drugs was to quickly induce a heart attack. There would undoubtedly be an autopsy, and the initial findings would be natural causes. A heart attack. The results of the toxicology tests would take about five days to be processed by the lab. The presence of digoxin would be noted. This would be confirmed by the fact that a bottle of the medication had been found in Tom's bathroom.

Clive returned to the sofa and sat down. If someone were to come to the door, he would instantly shout for help and open the door to let them in, announcing loudly that it looked like a heart attack.

He did not, however, expect anyone to come, so he was able to sit there and think through carefully how he would proceed. Of course, the longer he delayed, the more unlikely that any amount of CPR or use of a defibrillator, which undoubtedly a hotel of the eminence of Millbrook would have, would be able to revive the unfortunate Mr Shape.

Clive checked his watch. It had been fifteen minutes since he had felt no pulse. He had decided on his course of action.

He picked up the phone from the desk and dialled the emergency number, 111. The operator put him through to his requested service: ambulance. He explained who he was, where he was and that it looked like his friend had had a heart attack. He told her that he knew CPR and would start the process while waiting for them to arrive.

He then moved to the door, opened it and loudly yelled 'Help', leaving the door open. He returned quickly to Tom on the floor and proceeded to start CPR.

Beauford was the first to respond to the call. He had been about to head for the airport to oversee the final checks before the arrival of the president.

He quickly phoned for the medic that was part of the Secret Service team. Within a few moments, the medic arrived carrying a portable defibrillator kit. Ushering Clive out of the way, he ripped opened Tom's shirt and applied the pads. Despite repeated attempts, the shocks had no effect and Tom's body remained lifeless. When the ambulance team arrived the Secret Service medic informed them of the actions he had taken, and they took Tom's lifeless body out on a stretcher.

Chapter Thirty-Eight

It had been thirty minutes since the ambulance had taken Tom's body away. Charles had called an urgent meeting in the conference room. Beauford, the Secret Service doctor and the remaining six members of the APEC planning team were there. Jennifer Fletcher was visibly shocked. She had known Tom for many years. Despite his quirky ways, he had always looked out for her.

'I have just received an update from the hospital,' said Charles. 'They have confirmed that Tom was pronounced dead on arrival. I know a number of you tried to save Tom and I thank you for that. I have placed a guard on Tom's room with instructions that no one enters without my permission. The room will be treated as a crime scene until we can confirm otherwise.

'Of more immediate concern is the arrival of the US president in a little over five hours. Is that still currently the schedule, Beauford?'

'Subject to the outcome of this meeting it is, sir.'

'Quite,' said Charles. 'Clive, you were with Tom when the incident occurred. Do you have any reason to suspect it was other than natural causes?'

'I don't.'

'Does anyone else in the room have any reason to suspect it was other than natural causes?' asked Charles.

The room fell very silent. 'Thank you,' said Charles. 'Then please carry on.' Charles gestured to Beauford and Jennifer, 'May I have a word with you both?' The other occupants of the room took their cue and slowly filed out.

Charles suddenly realised that they had all been standing. It had just seemed right. He now motioned to Beauford and Jennifer to sit at the table. 'Jennifer, I am sorry for your loss. But the time constraints are harsh, and I need to ask whether you are able to step into the liaison role immediately.'

Jennifer looked at Charles for a moment. 'I have spoken with the Director General of the SIS, informed him of Tom's death and he has asked me formally to step into the lead liaison role. I feel able to do so.'

'Worst possible circumstances, but thank you for that,' said Charles.

Turning to Beauford, Charles said, 'I have had no indication from any quarter that Tom's death was anything but natural causes. Therefore, my recommendation, from the New Zealand side, is that the programme continues as planned. Are you of the same opinion?'

Beauford looked at Jennifer and Charles for a

moment. 'My condolences on your personal and country's loss,' he said to Jennifer. Then turning to Charles, 'I will call the head of the Secret Service and advise him of the situation. Based on everything we know so far, and the report of our medic who assisted in the resuscitation attempt, I will also be recommending that the programme continues as planned.'

'Right,' said Charles briskly, 'let us carry on then.'

I will need to recover Tom's service laptop and any files from his room, sir,' said Jennifer.

'Of course,' said Charles, 'let me make my call to the PM and I will join you at the room.'

Jennifer was waiting at Tom's room door. Only five minutes later Charles appeared. Charles addressed the police officer by the door. 'This is Ms Jennifer Fletcher of the SIS who will be recovering a laptop, phone and possibly some files. Please make a note of them when she leaves.' With that, Charles placed a sympathetic hand on Jennifer's shoulder before leaving her to enter the room.

While Charles was well aware this room was to be treated as a potential crime scene, it was not an option to leave an SIS secure phone and laptop and classified information lying around.

Jennifer closed the door behind her and stood for a moment. There were buttons on the floor from Tom's shirt when it had been ripped open to apply the defibrillator pads. The rest of the room was surprisingly tidy and quiet. It did not feel like a man, indeed her friend, had died in this room only an hour before. She shook herself from these thoughts and the professionalism and training kicked in.

Tom's secure mobile phone was by his bedside table. On the desk was his briefcase and laptop. She opened the case and flicked through the files inside. Nothing that she would not have expected him to have.

The laptop login had timed out and locked the device, as it should. She wondered what he had been looking at last. This thought grew larger, and she decided to find out.

She called the SIS's head of IT. At only about 300 staff strong, the New Zealand SIS is a small family and almost everyone knows everyone.

'Hi, Grainger,' said Jennifer when he answered the phone.

'I am very sorry to hear about Tom,' said Grainger. As head of IT, he was one of the first people to be informed if an SIS member of staff was no longer operative for any reason. Logins, passwords and clearances had to be instantly cancelled and phones and laptops wiped remotely.

'Thanks,' said Jennifer. 'I am in front of Tom's laptop, and I need to know what he was looking at last. Can you help?'

'Of course,' said Grainger. 'On deactivating Tom's account, the laptop itself has been wiped remotely so there is nothing on it now, but I can check the server logs to see what he was looking at.'

After only a moment, Grainger came back. 'He was reviewing the daily intel reports.'

'Which report did he look at last?' asked Jennifer.

'I can't see the actual report, but it is numbered AFG/2679852/2.'

Jennifer froze for a moment. As Tom's number two, she had also been reviewing all of the daily intel reports that Tom had. The AFG prefix indicated the report was out of Afghanistan. There had only been one report out of Afghanistan that she had reviewed that morning. This was the second report she had seen referring to the sale of a Stinger missile and a likely name of the buyer as 'The Aussie'.

She was jerked back from her thoughts by Grainger's voice on the phone. 'Are you still there, Jennifer?'

'Yes...' came the slow reply. 'That's all I need. Thanks, Grainger.'

'Take care of yourself, Jennifer and, again, sorry about Tom. Anything I can do to help, just ask.'

Jennifer pressed to disconnect the call and stared at the blank screen of Tom's laptop in front of her.

She reasoned that this was not evidence of anything untoward. Given the heightened state of anxiety of everyone to do with the Queenstown visit following Tom's death, if she even mentioned the words Stinger missile the balloon would well and truly go up. Should she report her findings up the chain or seek some actual evidence?

As she stared even more intently at the blank screen, she concluded that there were only two possibilities regarding Tom's death. One was the most unfortunate, but not impossible, timing of a heart attack. The second seemed very improbable.

She picked up the mobile again and called the Director General of the SIS. He was not going to like what she had to say.

Chapter Thirty-Nine

Clive's decision to resign from the army following APEC and the state visits was, he knew, the correct one. His leg injury was getting worse, and he knew that he would be assigned to ever-increasing stationary office-based duties. That was not why he had joined the army. He had booked his leave for immediately after the Queenstown state visit debriefing. He knew that if an unfortunate incident befell the US president, he might have to postpone his leave for a few weeks, but after the initial flurry of the inevitable enquiry, he would apply for medical retirement from the army. Then he was free to head off to meet up with Laura.

Clive joined Jennifer and Joe who were deep in discussion on one of the small bridges that span the ponds surrounding the main buildings of Millbrook Resort. It was 8 am and the sky was clear blue. The serene surroundings belied the buzz of activity and heightened anxiety around all those in the complex.

'Sorry for your loss, Jennifer,' said Clive.

'Yes, he will be a big loss as a friend and to the service,' said Jennifer.

'I must rush, but what can I do for you?'

'Did Tom say anything to you regarding what he was working on before he fell ill?'

'No, nothing,' said Clive. 'We were just talking generally and then he complained of a pain in his chest.'

'Where is the SAS anti-terrorism team located at the moment?' asked Jennifer.

'The two teams of four are with their two helicopters in a quiet corner of Queenstown Airport. They are ready for instant deployment. Do we have a problem?' Clive looked concerned.

'Possibly,' said Jennifer. 'What do you know about Stinger missiles?' She was watching his face intently. There was no reaction from Clive. Either her fears were unfounded or he was even better than she thought he was.

'Probably the best man-held surface-to-air missile available at the moment. Again, do we have an issue?'

'One was purchased in Afghanistan about six months ago,' said Jennifer. 'Just a little loose end for the intelligence community to follow up.'

'Okay, I need to be off then.'

With that Clive headed to the carpark. Jennifer and Joe remained on the bridge watching him go.

'Did you get what you wanted?' asked Joe.

'He heard what I wanted him to hear if that's what you mean,' said Jennifer.

'Did you get the tracker on his car?' Jennifer asked while still watching Clive walk away.

'Yes, I did and, as you asked, no one else is in the loop about what I've done. Oh, and what exactly am I doing by the way?'

Jennifer turned her gaze to Joe. 'In this very romantic setting you are helping the love of your life, darling.'

'Great, does that mean that if all of this goes even further south than we stand at the moment, we will be able to apply for adjoining cells?'

Changing back to her game face, Jennifer said, 'There are three people who know what we are doing at the moment. You, me and the Director of Intelligence. If, based on my hunch, we raise the issue of a Stinger missile now, two things will definitely happen. One, the president will instantly be spirited out of New Zealand. Second, if the ensuing investigation finds no evidence of any Stinger missile, I will be sacked and the Director will be asked to resign. You do not spoil the PM's party without at least some reasonable cause.'

With that, Jennifer started to walk to the carpark and casually looked over her shoulder to Joe. 'Thanks for the help. I can take it from here,' said Jennifer.

'Oh, no you don't,' said Joe, pulling alongside her. 'You have not signed for that tracker device so I had better keep a close eye on it.'

'But, your career...' Jennifer said before recognising

the determined look on his face. She knew better than to waste time trying to change his mind; she smiled and they both headed for her car.

As Jennifer settled in behind the wheel, Joe got into the passenger seat and opened his laptop.

'What is the range of the tracker?' asked Jennifer.

'It's a dual-access device,' answered Joe. 'Primarily it works off the mobile phone network. So, anywhere in the country where there is mobile phone coverage we are fine. If there is no mobile phone network, there is a transmitter function that will work for about three kilometres.'

They both watched as Clive pulled out in his car from the other side of the large carpark and headed off down the long drive to the exit of the hotel complex.

'So what you are saying is that if he heads towards Queenstown and the airport we are fine, but if he heads down the valley and into the wilds, with no mobile phone coverage, we had better not be too far away.'

'Yes, that's about it,' said Joe intently, not taking his eyes from the screen of his laptop.

Watching the display, the blinking dot that was Clive's car showed that he was now located at the end of the hotel drive. A couple of seconds later he said, 'He's turned right.'

Jennifer pulled slowly out of the carpark and headed down the driveway. As members of the planning team, the three of them had no fixed operational duties today. Their role was oversight and responding to any issues that might arise. So no one would miss any of them for a while.

As they progressed through the old historic gold-mining town of Arrowtown, Jennifer's mobile phone bleeped. She took it from her pocket and read the text. 'It's from the DG,' she said. 'Bill's jet has just left Auckland and it should arrive in Queenstown in about two hours.'

'Do you want me to call this in to Charles?' asked Joe.

Jennifer just turned and gave him a look.

Joe continued, 'Okay, I get it, we still have nothing and we carry on.' She smiled, nodded and drove on.

As they were leaving Arrowtown, the screen of Joe's laptop showed that Clive was approaching Arrow Junction.

'Where is he?' said Jennifer.

'Just approaching the junction,' said Joe. If he turns right, he is driving towards Queenstown and the airport. Left and he is heading up the valley. Next settlement the small village of Cromwell and,' Joe paused, 'he has turned left.'

They looked at each other.

'You might want to get a bit closer because I am pretty sure that until we get to Cromwell there will be no coverage and we may lose his signal.'

With that Jennifer sped up.

After a few moments, Joe exclaimed, 'What is he doing? He has turned onto the Crown Range road. Do you think he's having a day off sightseeing?'

'I really hope so.'

In a few minutes they had turned off the main road

and started up the Crown Range road – a very scenic route but full of dangerous hairpin bends. 'How far is he ahead?' asked Jennifer.

'About two miles as the crow flies, but I think that will translate into about eight road miles.'

They both looked up to see the road snaking its way up the side of the mountain. There was no other traffic. Very few people other than skiers would use this road in September.

'He seems to have stopped at the scenic lookout,' said Joe. 'Look, I know you want to get more proof, but the president of the USA will fly past here at low altitude in about sixty minutes. I think we need to call it in.'

'How?' said Jennifer. 'We are out of mobile phone coverage and, yes, we still do not have the slightest shred of evidence. We carry on.'

They stopped a couple of hundred metres short of the scenic lookout carpark. They could see only one car – Clive's. Jennifer took the small binoculars from the glove compartment and studied the car.

'I can't see Clive,' she said. She gave the binoculars to Joe. He also could only see the car and no sign of Clive.

'We don't have time to wait and see if he turns up. We need to find out if we have a problem,' said Jennifer. She opened a concealed panel in the driver's door of her car and extracted a Beretta automatic pistol. She removed the magazine, inspected it and reinserted it. Pulling back the slide, she placed a bullet in the barrel and then applied the safety catch. Joe just watched. This was not usual behaviour in his IT world.

'If I tell you to wait in the car, you are not going to, are you?'

'Nope,' said Joe.

'Okay, then let's see what our captain is up to,' said Jennifer. They both got out of the car, retrieved their jackets from the back seat and put them on quickly against the cold wind. Jennifer placed the small binoculars in one pocket of her jacket and the Beretta in the other.

They had decided to leave the car where it was and walk the 200 metres to the lookout so as not to alert Clive to their arrival. As they approached the lookout, all was quiet except for the steady noise of the icy wind. There was still no sign of Clive.

They arrived at the car and took one side each. They looked in through the windows into the front and back seats. Nothing of interest.

They inspected the lookout. At one end was a small path, more like a goat track. Joe surmised that it had been worn down by the more adventurous tourists for whom a picture from the safety of the well-presented lookout was not enough.

The path went down steeply from the lookout and then levelled out and swept around a very large bolder. Jennifer headed off down the track followed by Joe. To try to maintain a decent speed, given the urgency, they both instinctively put out their arms to help keep their balance on the steep slope.

This proved to be their undoing. Clive's timing was perfect. He stepped out from behind the bolder with a pistol levelled at Jennifer.

'Just keep on coming towards me and keep your hands out where they are at the moment.'

Both Jennifer and Joe skidded on the loose path gravel path but could do nothing but carry on down the track.

As they reached the part of the track where it levelled out, Clive called out, 'Stop there and keep your hands out.' They were now about five metres from Clive and hidden from anyone that might happen to drive down the road or stop at the lookout.

'I assume that you are armed, Jennifer, and that you are not, Joe. Automatic in your right jacket pocket, Jennifer, I assume.' Clive was not trying to show off. He was aiming to prove that he was in charge. The military-grade automatic pistol aimed at them more than confirmed this.

Without waiting for an answer, he said to Joe, 'Now I want you, very slowly, to put your left hand in Jennifer's right pocket and, with your forefinger and thumb, remove the gun and throw it on the ground by me. All very slowly.' Joe did as he was instructed.

'Now sit, please.' They both sat on the ground. Clive was well trained. He would never be closer than five metres to his captives and, if they made a dash for him, they would be dead before they covered half the distance.

'You killed Tom,' said Jennifer.

'Most unfortunate,' said Clive. 'I really did like him.

Now I need to ask, how much do you know, Jennifer? If I think you are lying to me, I will kill Joe and then ask you again.'

Jennifer thought for a moment. There was no upside to lying to Clive and there was really nothing extra that she knew that could assist him.

'My interest was tweaked when I confirmed that the last report that Tom reviewed was the sale of a Stinger missile in Afghanistan to someone called the "Aussie". Together with the timing of Tom's death, I went to the DG with my concern. We agreed that there was no evidence to suggest a Stinger missile was in New Zealand or that Tom's death was not natural causes. To even raise the suspicion at this stage would have the Secret Service spiriting the president out of the country and would spoil the PM's party. Big time. However, it couldn't just be left uninvestigated. As you were the last person to see Tom alive, you were the obvious one to investigate.'

'And Joe here?' Clive asked, casually swaying his gun at Joe.

'I urgently needed a tracking device to fit to your car. Joe had access to one.'

'So you are telling me that only you two and the DG know of your concern?' said Clive.

'That's correct,' said Jennifer. 'So what now?'

Clive did not answer. But reaching behind the large bolder, he retrieved a large pair of binoculars. Still holding the gun on his two captives, he raised the binoculars to his eyes and studied the mountains on the far side of the valley.

Both Jennifer and Joe followed the direction in which Clive's binoculars were pointed. They could both just make out a small white speck on the mountainside over the valley.

'So, that's the location of the person operating the Stinger,' said Joe. 'Makes sense to choose a close shot from above the jet.'

'So what happens to us after the jet goes down? The DG will know about my suspicions of you. If something happens to us, he will know it was you,' said Jennifer.

'Knowing is one thing, proving is something else. Tourists make a miscalculation on this road every year. Some of those miscalculations even prove to be fatal. Trying to prove that a car went over a cliff other than by accident can be quite tricky. Everyone is aware of your relationship and will assume you went out for a romantic drive over the Crown Range together. What a pity you were so distracted with each other and made a fatal mistake,' Clive smirked.

Their conversation was interrupted by a low rumbling noise. Unlike thunder, however, the noise was growing louder.

Then the three of them saw it. A small silver plane seeming to move so slowly as it flew down the valley, well below the mountain peaks on each side.

Without speaking, both Jennifer and Joe had contemplated making a dash towards Clive. Both had arrived at the same conclusion. They would probably be dead before they had fully stood up. That would be a waste. Even in the very remote chance that one of them got to Clive, it would not stop the missile being fired on the other side of the valley. They both felt completely helpless.

Chapter Forty

Laura had been waiting patiently but rather anxiously by the motorhome. She had watched the US Air Force transport aircraft fly past about an hour earlier. This confirmed that the next plane that flew past would have the call sign Air Force One.

She had placed the explosive device in the external cupboard of the motorhome beside the liquid propane gas cylinder. The timer had been set for four hours.

Her mind wandered to her long-time lover, Clive. They had first met when they had trained together during the joint New Zealand and Australia Army Officer course in Australia. They had stolen as much time together as they could over the intervening years. Since Clive's accident and her 'retirement', they had agreed that the time had come to start a new chapter of their lives together. The events of the next few minutes would ensure that it was a very rich one.

The Stinger missile unit was fully assembled and lying just inside the van door. She had been watching intently down the valley. There had been no air traffic for an hour now, a sure sign that the airspace had been closed to allow for the unimpeded passage of the VIP airplane.

All her senses fully heightened, she heard a noise long before the source came into view. She was surprised. It was not an airplane noise, as expected, but the sound of a motor vehicle. She tensed as the shape of an old Land Rover came up the track from the valley floor.

Like any good professional, Laura had made a number of different plans if she were interrupted at the small parking spot. These depended on how many people and at what time in her operation they showed up.

Given the imminent arrival of Air Force One, there was only one course of action for Laura. Turning her back to the now parking Land Rover, Laura took the pistol from her pocket and pulled back the slide to chamber the first round. Turning again to face the parking Land Rover some ten metres away, Laura moved her right hand holding the pistol behind her back. At the same time, as she moved towards the car, she smiled sweetly and waved with her left hand.

An elderly man was getting out of the driver's side and an elderly woman from the passenger door, both dressed for a day's hiking. Laura could see that there was no one else in the vehicle. Of all the times to choose to come hiking.

The man raised his arm to wave at Laura and cheerily said, 'Hello, we don't usually see many...' He did not finish his sentence as Laura put two bullets in quick succession into his chest. The woman had no time to react, or even move, before Laura put two bullets in her chest as well. Both were likely dead before they hit the ground, but years of training with special forces kicked in with Laura and she moved swiftly to each body in turn and put a single bullet in their heads.

Turning to look down the valley, she saw in the distance the small shape of a jet. She raised the binoculars for a second just to confirm it was a Gulfstream. Swiftly putting down the binoculars, she picked up the Stinger missile launcher and moved around the back of the motorhome. While it was a slim chance she would be spotted, there was no reason to expose herself shouldering a Stinger to the two pilots in the jet as it approached her.

As she had been practising, she would wait until the jet was alongside her and then shoulder the missile.

As the jet drew alongside her position, she estimated that it would be about 200 metres below her and about one kilometre away. This was a very short distance for a missile like the Stinger. She shouldered the missile and picked up the plane in the simple optical sights. Then she engaged the battery and gas unit that were an integral part of the device. She clicked the switch and could hear the beeping high-pitched tone as the guidance system in the rocket tried to pick up the heat signature from the

Gulfstream's twin jet engines. After only a few seconds, the tone went from a beep to a steady tone as the missile confirmed it had locked onto one of the engines of Air Force One.

Laura pulled the trigger to release the rocket and heard nothing. She would never hear anything again.

Chapter Forty-One

From the far side of the valley, Joe and Jennifer watched as the plane passed below the small white dot on the valley wall. Clive, with the pistol still aimed at them, also observed.

All waited, expecting to see the smoke trail of the Stinger missile as it left the location of the small white dot and streaked towards the silver jet that seemed to be moving so slowly now.

Jennifer and Joe wanted to cry out, but the situation seemed to be hopeless.

Then it happened. There was a large flash of light. All three of them assumed that this was the missile being fired and searched the space between the flash and the lumbering aircraft for a smoke trail or some indication of the missile's path.

As they searched, the jet continued unimpeded on its descent towards the airport, which was still out of sight.

There was then a second flash from the location of the white dot. This flash was even bigger than the first. What was happening? Could this be a second missile, they all wondered?

But, unlike the first flash, the second did not die away. It got brighter and, even in the daylight, it was clearly visible. Something was on fire.

They all turned their attention back to the jet, which was almost out of sight. It had continued flying on its slow path, unaffected and unhindered.

Clive's heart was racing. He levelled his pistol at his two captives. They and he noticed that his hand was not as steady as it had been. He raised his binoculars to his eyes again and what he saw confirmed his worst fears. The white outline of the motorhome that he had previously been able to observe with the binoculars was gone. It had been replaced by a bonfire of flame.

Clive was mystified and distraught. He had no idea what had happened. What had caused the first explosion? Presumably, the second explosion had involved the explosive incendiary device that he knew Laura was going to place in the motorhome.

No one at that location could have survived. He lowered the binoculars from his eyes. He looked at Jennifer and Joe, but he did not really see them.

Laura was gone. The lifestyle they had talked of and dreamed of for years was gone. The only person he had ever truly loved, ever since they both met as twenty-year-old army officer cadets all those years ago. All gone.

Jennifer was watching Clive's face intently. The poker face had gone completely. This was not just the distress of a failed operation. This was more. This was personal, she realised. Possibly she could use that.

In the calmest voice she could muster she said, 'It's over Clive. The president is safe and whoever was on the other side of the valley is gone. You need to let us take you in.'

The words only just penetrated Clive's mind through the mist of all his other thoughts.

It was all over, finished. There was nothing left. When they identified Laura, and they would even if it was from dental records or DNA, the link with him would be established from army records and the fellow officers who had seen them together over the years. He had also killed Tom and the SIS would not rest until they got him.

It was finished. He was finished.

He looked again at Jennifer and Joe, the pistol now by his side. This time, neither considered making a sudden move.

Clive looked at Jennifer and said, 'I really am sorry about Tom,' and with that he placed the barrel of the pistol under his chin, pulled the trigger and sent a bullet through his brain which exited through the top of his head.

Chapter Forty-Two

Jennifer had left Joe with Clive's body while she drove back on the Crown Range road in search of a mobile phone signal. She found one at the turnoff with the main road, pulled over and called the Director General.

She related what had transpired. The DG listened carefully, not interrupting, before asking two questions.

'Are you and Joe okay?'

'Yes, unhurt,' said Jennifer.

'Do we have any reason at all to suspect that there remains a threat to any VIP?'

'No, sir.'

'Then this is how we shall proceed. I am going to despatch one of the SAS teams to secure the missile firing site. Then I am going to have the local police block the Crown Range road ten kilometres either side of the scenic viewing location. They will be told that it is because of a serious road accident. I will then despatch a second SAS team in their helicopter to rendezvous with you at the viewing point. You are to return there, meet up with Joe and I will contact you shortly on the SAS's secure helicopter radio comms with further instructions. Is that clear, Jennifer?'

'Yes, sir.'

Jennifer headed back up the Crown Range road again and, as she got to one of the hairpin turns near the first section, she could see the flashing lights of a stationary police car at the bottom of the road closing it off. She thought that this was probably a routine occurrence for the police, given the difficulty of navigating the road. They would be thinking that it was just another tourist who had underestimated the tightness of the hairpin bends.

Chapter Forty-Three

It had been a very late night for Jennifer and Joe. They had managed to get in a few hours' sleep in their Millbrook hotel rooms. However, both had been woken early requesting their presence at a breakfast meeting with the DG in one of the more out-of-the-way houses on Millbrook Estate. Golf carts, the standard mode of transport around the estate, had been waiting to whisk them to the villa, only ten minutes after the telephone calls.

The DG had arrived in Queenstown from Wellington by private jet. As the airport only operates during daylight hours, he had had to wait for the sun to come up before he could travel.

When Joe arrived at the villa, Jennifer was already seated at a large table, set with a continental breakfast, orange juice and coffee.

Joe was ushered into the room by the man posted at the door.

'Good morning, Mr Edwards,' said the man who approached him across the room. With his hand outstretched, he went on, 'I don't believe we have met before. My name is Damian Brown and I am, for my sins, the Director General of Intelligence. Please have a seat and help yourself to breakfast and coffee.'

Joe sat next to Jennifer and poured himself a coffee.

'You may not have had a chance to look at the newspaper this morning. I suggest that you look at page one and then there are two small stories on pages three and four.' He handed both Jennifer and Joe a copy of the local newspaper, the *Otago Sentinel*. He then helped himself to breakfast while he waited for them to read the articles.

They both read page one. It was dominated by a press release from the White House. It was a question-and-answer press session following the president's golf round with Burton Shipley, husband of the New Zealand prime minister.

Q: How was your golf game today, Mr President? Did it improve as you went along?

THE PRESIDENT: It got a lot better. It had nowhere to go but up when I started. No, we did better and we won the match, thanks mostly to my partner here. But we did okay. We played the way partners should play. When I had a good score, he didn't; when he had a good score, I didn't play good. We wasted no shots.

MR SHIPLEY: The President suggested at one stage that we were playing very good brother-in-law golf. I thought the line was very good.

THE PRESIDENT: We did, we actually played the pro and his partner, and we won – and they bought me a Diet Coke. It was a big stake here, it was great.

Q: What did you think of the course, Mr President?

THE PRESIDENT: It's fabulous, it's really quite a wonderful course. It's an honest course. It's a good course, it plays hard, but it's an honest course.

Q: What do you think of Queenstown?

THE PRESIDENT: I wish I had weeks to spend here. You know, when we were coming in the airplane, landing, everybody on our plane was just gasping when we saw the landscape. It's just so beautiful. You're all very fortunate.

Joe did not need to read any more of that article and he turned to page three.

'Another Death on Crown Range road.

'Police had to seal off the Crown Range road yesterday following another fatal accident. The New Zealand Defence Force has confirmed that a member of the Army was killed when his car left the road and fell into a ravine. The name of the soldier will not be released until the next of kin has been informed. Calls have again been made by the Queenstown Lakes District Council to improve safety on the road.'

Joe then turned to page four.

'Tourist and Two Locals Die in Motorhome Explosion

'Police have confirmed that a tourist and two well-known locals have died in the explosion of a motorhome. The explosion, which was seen by several passing motorists on State Highway 6, occurred on a remote track above the Kawarau River, just outside Queenstown. No cause of the explosion has been confirmed, but it is common for this type of motorhome to use an LPG gas bottle for cooking. Due to the remote location of the accident, a Defence Force helicopter has been utilised to remove the wreckage of the motorhome and the three bodies. They will be taken to a secure location for further analysis regarding the cause of the accident. No details of the identity or nationality of the tourist have been released, pending the notification to their relatives.'

When Joe looked up from the paper, Jennifer was looking at him and the DG was eating a croissant. He finished, put down his plate and took a very deliberate sip of coffee.

'You will appreciate that, after such a successful APEC and state visit by the President of the United States, there is little appetite for a significant distraction. It is felt by people in high places that there is little to be gained by full disclosure.'

The DG paused to see if either Joe or Jennifer wished to say anything. When they did not, he continued. 'I have been informed that there is not much left of the motorhome but that some parts of a Stinger missile have been recovered. While the explosion and extreme fire make identification very difficult, parts of an individual have been recovered. Presumably the Stinger missile operator. The two locals, who were found a short distance from the motorhome wreckage, appear to have stumbled across the plot. They were both shot at close range.'

Looking directly at Joe, the DG said, 'I am sure that I don't need to remind you both that this is now a national security matter and you are not to speak of it to anyone.'

'Of course, sir,' replied Joe.

As the DG moved to take another sip of coffee, Joe asked, 'Just one question, if I may?'

The DG paused with coffee cup in mid-air. 'I will answer it if I am able.'

'Is there any indication as to why the Stinger missile exploded?'

'None at this stage,' replied the DG. 'It is possible that we may never get a definitive answer as to whether it was an error by the operator or a malfunction due to the age of the device. Additionally, the manner in which it has been transported, stored and maintained could be significant. Or indeed, there may be some other reason.'

'Do we know if there were any accomplices other than Captain Robertson?' asked Jennifer.

The DG thought for a moment. 'We are not aware of any accomplices at the moment. It is felt that to conduct a detailed investigation might bring unwarranted attention to the incident. It is, therefore, felt most appropriate to allow the unfortunate demise of the captain in a driving mishap, and the death of the motorhome tourist in an accident, to stand.'

With that the DG rose from his chair.

'I have another meeting to go to now, but, please, finish your breakfast before you leave.'

With that he left the room and Joe and Jennifer found themselves alone with their thoughts.

'I need a walk,' said Jennifer.

'Would you like some company?'

'Always.'

Chapter Forty-Four

It was a week since the well-publicised golf game in Queenstown. Captain Alex Conrad was clearing his desk at the barracks of the Australian SAS in Swanbourne, Perth, Western Australia. He looked at the framed photograph of his brother, in full dress uniform, on his desk. After a moment's reflection, he placed the photo in his bag. This was his brother who had died four years before in a helicopter crash in Afghanistan. The helicopter had been downed by a Stinger missile.

Two days earlier, he had obtained a copy of the 15 September issue of the *Otago Sentinel* newspaper. The two small stories on pages three and four had confirmed the successful outcome of his planned course of action. Later that day he had put in his papers to leave the army. With his accumulated leave, he had been able to depart immediately.

As he looked around the office for the last time, he

asked himself the same question he had posed many times over the last few months. Had he booby-trapped the Stinger missile to explode when fired because of the death of his brother to one of those missiles? Or was it for the money that was now going to give him a very comfortable retirement, with no loose ends to worry about? As he left the office for the final time, he thought either was a very good reason.

Chapter Forty-Five

It was now January 2000 in Gstaad, Switzerland and the New Year celebrations around the world had completed and a new millennium had begun. The chateau in the alps was large and very old. It had been in the family of the Swiss owner for generations. It was over three hours by car to the city of Basel on the Rhine where the corporate headquarters of the pharmaceutical company, of which he was chairman, was located. This distance did not matter to the chairman as his personal helicopter would travel the distance in much less time.

The helicopter had been busy that day. It had met private jets that had landed at Geneva, Zurich and Bern airports and ferried the three passengers directly to the chateau.

The local area around Gstaad at this time of year was full of winter sports enthusiasts. But for the four men who now stood in the large lounge room looking at the picture-perfect mountains covered in snow, skiing was not on their minds.

One year on from their previous meeting, it was the turn of the Swiss host to hand out the brandy. The meal which they had just finished had, of course, been excellent.

'Well, gentlemen,' said the host in his Swiss German-accented English. 'We seem to find ourselves back in the same position we were in over two years ago. The leaders' communiqué agreed at the Auckland APEC meeting commits the twenty-one countries to even greater cooperation and the march for globalisation goes on.

'As does the international risk to our drug patents and the wave of cheap generic drugs produced by Asian countries. Do we try again at the next APEC meeting?' This comment and question had come from the man from the southern states of the US.

'Perhaps we need to consider another option?' injected the man from Connecticut. 'Rather than try to topple the march to globalisation from the outside, I wonder if it would be possible to destroy it from the inside?'

'Go on,' said the fourth man in the room.

'Well, we are all extremely aware of the power of money in the US presidential elections. We have each of us for years, both separately and, on occasions, in collaboration, applied our considerable financial resources, via various lobbying efforts, to obtain favourable business goals in return for large political donations.'

He took a sip of his brandy and they all waited for him to continue.

'What if we could identify a US presidential candidate who could be moulded to hold our anti-globalisation position? With the right individual, we could apply our financial resources to place them in a position to win the party nomination and, ultimately, the Presidential election. Our man, or woman, would then be able to dismantle the march to globalisation and replace it with a much more nationalistic stance. This would, of course, be a major advantage to all of us.'

'It would require considerable skill and time to identify and then groom such a candidate,' added the man from the southern states. 'Is it even practical?'

The room fell quiet as each of them regarded the snowy vista before them.

The silence was broken by the host. 'Maybe we should ask our guest?' He picked up a small, handcrafted Swiss bell from the table and rang it. He hardly had time to replace the bell on the table before an immaculately dressed servant entered the door of the lounge and stood awaiting his instructions.

'Would you ask Mr Butler to join us, please?'

About the Author

Mike grew up in the UK but has lived in New Zealand for the past thirty years. His background in information technology and security led him in 1999 to head the New Zealand Police's IT and communications for a meeting of world leaders, including US President Bill Clinton. Holding top-secret security clearance, he coordinated with intelligence agencies and police forces around the world. For the following two decades, Mike was one of New Zealand's foremost computer forensic scientists and expert witnesses, cofounding his own company.

Excited by a lifetime of working in crime and technology, he wrote this novel based on his first-hand knowledge. He now lives in the Bay of Islands, New Zealand with his wife Sue, when not pursuing his passion for world travel.

Contact Mike at mikespenceauthor@gmail.com
www.facebook.com/authorMikeSpence

Acknowledgments

My wife Sue, first reader, and for putting up with me for so many years.

Martin Taylor for publishing assistance and Brian O'Flaherty for editing and proofreading. My friend 'Tom', R.I.P. You can't put a price on liaison.

And finally, the women and men of the New Zealand Police. Probably the finest police force in the world.